TORCH SONGS FOR THE DEAD

JASON CHANCE BOOK 3

JOSH GRIFFITH

STREET PRESS

PART I

EQUINOX

1

Before the vehicle reached the end of the long drive, I knew its driver brought bad news. Whoever was behind the wheel didn't seem to care about the potholes that made the tan-colored SUV bounce up and down like an off-roader racing across mountainous terrain. The driver went so fast and took the turns in the dirt road so sharply that the truck threatened to roll over several times. This driver came with purpose, an agenda. My gut told me it wasn't something I wanted to hear.

I had been sitting on the cabin porch for the better part of an hour, sipping a glass of bourbon while looking at nothing more than the sun setting over the hills. Now, the fiery sphere hovered just above the Pacific, kissing the horizon, no longer strong enough to make me squint. "Blue," the final track from R.E.M.'s final album *Collapse into Now*, blared from a set of speakers in the open window, the volume too high for anyone except me. I hadn't expected company when I turned it on and came outside.

The dirt-streaked truck rounded the last curve of the driveway before arriving at the cabin, kicking up dust and grit in its wake. As it did, I got my first clear view of the man behind the wheel through the windshield. I wasn't all that surprised to see him; part of me had been expecting and dreading his visit for two months.

I placed my drink on a side table and stood, the dull pain in my knee sharpening as I straightened. I had sustained injuries over much of my body during my last investigation as a homicide detective for the LA Sheriff's Department. They had begun to heal during my elected isolation, and I no longer needed to walk with a cane, but stiffness and pain still made sitting for long stretches uncomfortable, standing even more so. I had come up to Santa Barbara with my daughter, Kathy, and Charley Frasier (my ex-lover and ex-partner turned lover again) to recuperate. We all had wounds to heal, and we had stayed off the grid for eight weeks. Until today.

I took a few steps toward the front of the porch, steadying myself by holding onto a post that supported the overhanging roof of a cabin built almost a hundred years before. I watched as the SUV came to a stop. The driver left the motor running while he took off his sunglasses and set them on the dash. Then he cut the engine and got out, looking over at me across the dirty hood. He was dressed casually in jeans and a UCLA T-shirt under a lightweight windbreaker.

"You're a hard man to find," he said.

"Apparently not too hard. How did you find me?"

"Give me a little credit." My sheriff's department boss, Captain Ellison came around the vehicle and climbed the two creaking steps to the weathered wood porch. "You don't look as bad as I expected."

"I guess it's all perspective," I said.

"Isn't everything?" He held out his hand, and I shook it. "How's Kathy?"

"Better. Stronger every day."

"Good. And you?"

"Knee's feeling okay. The gashes on my scalp are healing. The pain in my shoulder and elbow is mostly gone."

"That's all good to hear," he said, "but not what I meant."

"No, I figured it wasn't."

Ellison nodded toward the glass of whisky on the table. "Think I could get one of those?"

"Depends. Why are you here, Germaine?"

If it surprised him to hear me call him by his first name and not *Captain*, he didn't let on.

"You expect me to believe you don't already know?" he said.

"I told you when I left I needed time," I said. "I'm up here for reasons that have nothing to do with the department. Or even solely with me."

"And I appreciate what those reasons are. That's never been the issue."

"Then what is? Why'd you track me down?"

"There are things we need to talk about. To clarify."

"If it's about the Caligula case, I've got nothing more to add to what I told you before I left. Everything of importance I know was in my notes." Caligula was the last investigation I'd worked as a homicide detective for the department.

Ellison frowned, covering his top lip with his bottom one. The bright white of his eyes around gray irises made a vibrant contrast to his dark complexion. He had shaved off the signature mustache he'd had as long as I had known him, and his salt-and-pepper hair, usually cropped short, had grown out since I had last seen him. The changes made him look younger. That probably was his intention. Maybe he had seen the years in his face when he looked in the mirror, and they scared him. I encountered the same ghost myself, staring back at me every morning.

"There are still a lot of questions," he said. "And I've got a few things I'd like to run by you. Listen to what I have to say. You can always tell me to fuck off once I'm finished."

I laughed. "As long as that's an option." I saw the hint of a smile on his lips, but the look in his eyes disturbed me.

"I'll get you that drink," I said and went inside.

It was a small cabin—two bedrooms, a living room, kitchen, and one bath—in the hills above Goleta, north of Santa Barbara. The place was an old fire rangers' stopping point from the 1930s through the early '70s. Budget cuts forced the park service to close it down in '75 and put it on the market. My father, Scotty Chance, a detective with the narcotics bureau of the sheriff's department, bought it cheap, then spent a year and a half turning it from a shack into a livable home. It sat isolated on a large field high above the sea, with a view from the porch all the way to the Channel Islands. The water from its faucets flowed fresh and cold. Although it had no air conditioning, the exposed pine walls kept the rooms cool on even the hottest days, with the help of large ceiling fans. The kitchen appliances were what some might call vintage—I called them old—but they worked.

When I was a child, my father and I often came up on weekends, and I had brought Kathy at least twice a year since she was born. She was now approaching eighteen. After the recent horror she had experienced at the hands of an evil man at the center of the Caligula case, she chose to come to this place to recover and heal.

I fixed Ellison a drink—two fingers' worth of Michter's American Whiskey—and topped off my glass, adding ice to both. It was the end of the day, and I had nothing pressing except to find out why my old captain had driven two hours to see me. Part of it, I knew, related to those loose ends of the Caligula mess dangling back in LA, but Ellison's *I've got a few things I'd like to run by you* and *Listen to what I have to say* implied something other than the old case. Something new.

Returning to the porch, I handed Ellison the glass, then eased back down into my chair. He sat opposite me on the porch swing. He took a sip of the bourbon.

"Good stuff," he said.

"Only the best for you."

He puckered his lips and rocked back and forth in the swing seat, pushing against the porch floor with the balls of his feet. The chains squeaked, sounding like the soft cries of a cat. "Is your daughter inside?"

"No, she's in town with Charley, picking up some things."

Ellison's face registered surprise. "Charlotte's here too?"

"Yeah, we're trying things out. Again."

"Well, that's good news. Damned good news indeed." He raised his glass to me. "I hope it works out this time."

"As do we."

Off above the trees, two ravens swooped and sailed around each other, squawking as they disappeared over the crest of a hill. A wind picked up, coming in off the ocean. It felt cooling in the heat of the afternoon and smelled of salt water and pine. "They'll be awhile. You can talk freely," I said.

Ellison set his glass down on a side table. "You left us with a lot of questions."

"I'm sorry about that, but I had more important things to focus on—like the wellbeing of my daughter. You know that. And I handed over all my notes on the investigation to Harry Feiffer." Just thinking about the case again made my stomach tighten.

"I'm not here to lay blame," Ellison said. "I understand why you needed to get away. We all do." He shook his head. "What a mess of a case. Caligula, Jesus. Even the fucking name."

"The bastards probably thought it was cute."

"Those bastards are the loose ends I'm talking about."

"One of them got what he deserved."

"JoJo Sellars, I know. But the other one's gone missing. Derek Vanderbrook."

I shrugged. "Sometimes they get away." I wasn't about to tell Ellison I knew exactly what had happened to Vanderbrook, nor was I going to reveal my direct involvement in his demise. Why open an ugly Pandora's box that might never get closed? I wasn't ready to confess my complicity. The investigation was one of the most despicable cases I had ever worked, and it had almost killed my daughter. I did what I felt I had to to put an end to everything. For every cop, there comes a point when you have to say *enough* and let things go. Otherwise, you tempt madness.

"I have no idea where he is," I said. "I did what I could to end things. JoJo is dead. The women were found and rescued. Kathy is healing. That's all that matters. I'm just trying to forget."

Ellison leaned forward. "Derek's father, Jensen, is offering a reward for any information as to his son's whereabouts. Three million dollars if the son is found." The Captain referred to Jensen Vanderbrook, a billionaire real estate developer with a questionable history. His son had preyed on vulnerable women.

"That's a lot of money," I said.

"And a bounty that will give incentive to a lot of wackos to come forward with information. Most of it will be bogus and will waste our time."

"For sure."

"I was hoping you would just tell me what really happened, and we could avoid all the bullshit."

"What makes you think I know more than I've said?"

"Because of the way you left things. Vague. Dismissive. That's not like you. Look, I get it. I understand. You probably had to cross some lines to get things done. Hell, it wouldn't be the first time one of us has had to do something ... questionable."

"Somehow, I doubt you ever have."

He waved a hand. "No one would blame you, a case like that. I just need to know what to expect. What to prepare for. I don't want to be blindsided if Vanderbrook sues the department or worse."

I sympathized with Ellison's need. It pained me to keep him in the dark. But I wasn't ready. Not yet. I looked off toward the ocean to avoid his impatient stare. The sun had sunk halfway below the horizon, and the moon was a glowing sphere in the darkening sky above the hills to the south. A coyote howled in the distance at the approaching night.

"I've got nothing to tell you," I said at last. "I'm sorry."

He scowled. "Why are you acting this way, Jason? I've been your supporter for a hell of a lot of years. You're the one who kept secrets from me on this last one. You shut me out. You betrayed my trust."

"Obviously, we see events differently."

"Respect should go both ways."

"It's unfortunate you took my actions as a slap in your face. They weren't meant to be. I did what I had to do to protect my daughter."

"And thank God she's safe. We all want to move on, like she has. Like you have. Other cases. Other crimes. You know the drill."

With that comment, I knew his talk about Caligula had merely been an intro. A prologue. Ellison was setting me up, trying to lay guilt on me. He didn't care that I had left things unanswered with the last case or might have broken some rules to close it. He wanted me to feel like I owed him because he needed something else from me.

"You've made your point," I said. "I get it now. And you've got me curious. What's this other crime you just referred to?" When he hesitated, I added, "Get to it, Captain. Why are you really here?"

Ellison stared at me, wetting his lips. "Something's happened, Jay. Something bad."

He stood, went down the porch steps, walked over to his car, and opened the passenger door. From the seat, he picked up a manila envelope. The packet was smooth and clean, free of smudges and wrinkles. Returning to the porch swing, he pulled out a stack of papers from the envelope. The clip holding the documents together slid off in his large hand. He shuffled through the documents and photographs. When he found the picture he wanted, he handed it to me.

I wasn't prepared for what I saw. That, too, probably was Ellison's intention. He wanted to shock me, working every nerve and angle he could to produce a response in me. It worked. I felt a stirring in my belly, a sensation I hadn't experienced in many months—the jolt of adrenaline that always hits at the beginning of an investigation. It was an instinct as common to detectives as breathing.

In the 8x10 crime scene photograph, the remains of three people—one male adult, one female adult, and a small child—were seated side by side against a wall partially destroyed by fire. They were on their knees, their arms twisted behind their backs. The plasterboard behind them had been scorched through, exposing partially destroyed 2x4 studs. The family's bodies were seared down to the bone in most areas, though a few spots of skin remained, red and blistering.

"Jesus," I muttered.

"And then some."

"Why are their hands behind their backs? Were they tied up?"

Ellison nodded. "Look at their necks."

Because of the severity of the burns, it took me a moment to see what he meant: each victim had a deep laceration on the throat, a gaping wound caked with blood blackened by the fire. Their throats had been slit.

The image was brutal. Nightmarish.

"Who are they?" I asked.

"The family's name is Horton. Dale and Jackie. Their daughter is Abigail. She was ten years old."

At hearing the names, my jaw tensed. I tried to swallow, but my mouth had gone dry. I reached for my glass and drank most of the bourbon down. "I know them," I said, so softly I barely heard my own voice.

"I figured. And you know the place too."

Indeed, I did. 2675 Laurel Avenue. The house where I grew up.

2

"When did it happen?" I asked.

"Two days ago," Ellison said. "A neighbor called in the fire around 10 p.m."

"I'm assuming you haven't caught whoever did this."

"No, but there's more." He pulled another photo from the stack. "This one isn't gruesome. It's of the house."

He handed me the police shot of my old backyard, taken near the retaining wall. The photographer faced the building, using a wide-angle lens that took in all of the yard and the half-destroyed house. I hadn't lived there for many years, but seeing the destruction, the violation of the place where I had spent much of my life, tore me up inside. Images of random memories flooded through my mind: afternoon barbecues on the back deck, playing catch with my dad while steaks and burgers sizzled on the grill; swinging on an old tire my dad hung for me on the thick branch of the maple tree that stretched over onto our property from next door; lying in the grass at night with June Gooding when we were barely thirteen, holding hands and counting stars.

That lawn, once so lush and green, had been defiled,

dug up in at least a half-dozen places, each hole two feet wide and three feet deep. "Somebody was searching for something," I said.

"The floorboards throughout the house were also torn up."

"Looking for what?"

"That's the question. The Hortons were clean. No arrests. No suspicious behavior. No hint of trouble on either side, going back two generations. Nothing."

I remembered the family. I sold them the house a few months after my father died. A good couple. Happy. Excited about their first home. The daughter, Abigail, was then barely four years old. Now dead. Tied up and slaughtered. Why? To be interrogated? The killer wanted something in the house. What?

Ellison took a document from the pile of papers and read from it. "Three days ago, Alex Davis, Armando Trujillo, Colin Parker, and Paula Ramirez were released from prison."

I knew these names: my dad's narcotics crew. *The Four Horseman of the Apocalypse*, he called them. They were arrested eight years ago, charged with conspiracy, extortion, bribery, perjury, robbery, and trafficking—all done under the blanket of undercover investigative work. Their arrests came after a two-year investigation, a joint effort between the FBI, federal prosecutors, and the sheriff's internal affairs unit. All were convicted.

Everyone on the team but Scotty Chance.

No evidence ever linked my father to any of their crimes, and they testified in his favor, claiming that he was clean, and they had kept him in the dark, working behind his back all those years. I remember how heavily their arrests weighed on him. He had considered them to be friends, as well as colleagues, and their betrayal broke his heart. A year after the indictments came down, he shot himself with a handgun in the kitchen of our Laurel Avenue home. He was 56 years old. He left me a note saying he'd seen enough. Dad's death hit me hard. To this day, I have trouble dealing with investigations involving suicide.

"You remember their last case?" Ellison asked. "The one right before they got busted."

I did. They had targeted Yuri Petrov, a Russian-born, LA-based opioid trafficker. Colin Parker infiltrated his ring and, while undercover, dug up enough dirt for an arrest and conviction. Petrov went down around the same time the team did, sentenced to life without parole.

"Is Petrov still in jail?" I asked.

"Nope, escaped six months ago. Nobody knows where he is."

"Didn't money go missing at the time of the arrest? Five million or something? And a few kilos of heroin?"

"All rumor, never proved," Ellison said. "The DA wanted to add it to the charges against your father's men, but there was no evidence they took anything from Petrov."

"Still, maybe it wasn't a rumor. If Yuri escaped, maybe he's looking for his money and drugs."

"Word is he's disappeared into Mexico."

"Doesn't make it true," I said. "He could be holed up in Torrance, for all we know. Five million in cash and smack with a street value of another two. Wouldn't you want it back? And if he's in Mexico, he could have people working for him Stateside, trying to find it."

"So you agree the house was the target," Ellison said, "not the family. Somebody was looking for something they believed was there. In the home of Scotty Chance, the one guy who didn't go down."

"Every single member of my father's team testified to his innocence."

"You know we've got to ask, Jay. It's an obvious assumption."

"Again, doesn't make it true." I looked down and saw I had balled my hands into fists. I took a breath to relax. "Any indication the killers found what they were after?"

"They didn't. They're still looking."

"How do you know that?"

"Colin Parker's house burned to the ground early this morning. Torn apart first. We found his body inside, burnt to a crisp." Ellison handed me yet another photo. In this one, the remains of a badly burned body lay in the center of a shell of a bedroom. "I don't much like Petrov for this," he said. "He's got $75 million parked in various offshore accounts. Probably twice that in liquid, spread across Russia and South America. Why take such risk and expense for a few million more?"

"Because it's not about the money. My dad's team brought him down. It's revenge. Money's just icing on the cake."

"I don't see him taking the chance either way."

"Maybe not," I said and handed Ellison back the photo. A headache had come on, just behind my eyes, caused by a combination of heat, too much bourbon, and memories of my past. "So what do you want from me?"

"Come back, and help us. You have a special connection to this one, which gives you a special understanding of the situation."

"Why? Because my old house got burned down? Because my father's colleagues turned out to be dirtbags? Or is it because you think my dad was one of those dirtbags?"

"I'm not passing judgment on Scotty, but others might. Wouldn't you like to make sure his name stays clean?"

"I shouldn't have to." My headed pounded. Ringing had started in my ears. "Sorry. The answer's no."

Ellison scowled, placing the photos back with the other documents. "Then I guess that's that." He took the paperclip from his pocket, used it to secure the stack, and returned everything to the manila envelope.

"I'm not trying to be an asshole," I said. "I buried my father six years ago. His sins went with him to the grave. And I'm not ready to come back to work. I'm sorry you wasted a trip."

"Me too." Ellison stood up. "Thanks for the drink."

I didn't want to leave things on a sour note. He had come here to give me an opportunity to protect my father's name and memory. That counted for something. "Charley and Kathy will be home soon," I said. "I need to get dinner started. You're welcome to stay. I know Charley would love to see you."

"Thanks, but no. I've got to get back. The DA's all over my ass on this one because of the department connection." This was a last attempt to make me feel guilty. I stayed silent, refusing to give in. He held out his hand. I shook it, and we said our goodbyes.

In the kitchen, I poured the remaining booze and ice from our drinks into the sink, rinsed both glasses, and set them aside—all just to be doing something. I felt angry but still couldn't blame Ellison. He had made no accusations. He was doing his job. Positing theories. Exploring all the angles of a case that needed solving before someone else got hurt.

As I shut the tap water off, I heard the front screen door squeak open then slam shut. A moment later, Ellison's car engine revved. His tires crunched on the gravel as he drove off, back down the hill toward the main highway. I went into the living room. The manila envelope lay on the coffee table. Ellison had scribbled my name across the front in neat, precise handwriting. His card, with his private cell number written under the printed office line, was clipped to the corner. I grabbed the envelope and shoved it into an end-table drawer, refusing to let him drag me back.

But as I prepared dinner, waiting for Charley and Kathy to return, I couldn't get the brutal images of the Horton family out of my mind.

3

Trane sat behind the wheel of his black-on-black 2003 BMW M5, drinking a cup of wretched coffee he had bought at a gas-station food mart in Calabasas. He watched as Sylvia Davis pulled into the open garage of the house across the street. She parked next to a midnight-blue Porsche 911.

Alex's ride, Trane thought. *I'll be damned. She kept it for him all these years.*

Trane turned up the radio, the gentle sounds of Oliver Nelson's "Stolen Moments" filling the car. Sylvia headed across the lawn to the front door, carrying a to-go bag from a local deli. She wore a short skirt and loose blouse.

She's aged some. A little heavier in the hips, a sag to her shoulders. Still attractive, though. Trane had lusted after her back in the day, as much out of rivalry with Alex as any real attraction. Trane teased himself that maybe he would have some fun with her tonight after he dealt with her husband.

Stop it. That's foolish mind play. Mental masturbation.

He had no time for that. Not now. Tonight, he was on a mission.

Trane leaned back on the headrest to wait. The neighborhood was quiet, peaceful, with a few people out walking their dogs and strolling along the sidewalks. Most windows glowed with the amber light and flicker of television screens. People at home, enjoying their cocktails and overpriced dinners, living their fat, comfortable lives in cool, comfortable houses they probably couldn't afford.

"Stolen Moments" gave way to Coltrane's "Equinox." Trane smiled. This was hands-down his favorite piece by his favorite artist. Coltrane, the master. Hearing his namesake—the man for whom he had given himself a nickname—always thrilled him. Bird, Dex, Miles, all were good —hell, better than good; most times, they were great—but Coltrane was a genius among geniuses. A musical god, with talent that soared to a whole other level. His playing wasn't just emotional; it was spiritual.

When he was just ten years old, after his father had given him his first serious beating, Trane locked himself in his room and turned up Coltrane's "Giant Steps" as loud as it would go, so no one would hear him cry. At fifteen, he lost his virginity to "Body and Soul," playing on repeat. When he first killed a man, Trane sought solace in the *Ballads* album, listening to it until his shaking and nausea subsided.

Violence, sex, and murder had become second nature to him—the pain of brutality and the angst and illness caused by killing were no longer issues for him, nor did the acts require solace—but his love of Coltrane endured. It was a drug for him. *No, an elixir.* A potion of magical powers that gave him peace and strength to face and endure whatever was necessary to achieve a goal.

Trane looked over at the house. He would let Alex and Sylvia have their drinks then start their dinner. Relaxing. Settling in. Dropping their guard while they devoured their deli and perhaps got engrossed in some movie or TV show. It was important to make his move at the optimum time. Not too early, not too late. The *right* time, so he'd have the upper hand.

SYLVIA TOOK THE WRAPPED TURKEY SANDWICH AND THE Chinese chicken salad container from the takeout bag and set them on the kitchen island. The TV blared in the family room—Alex, watching CNN. It was disconcerting to hear noises in the house again. After he went to prison, she didn't watch television or listen to the radio. The first few weeks, she shut down completely, as depressed and devastated as someone who had lost a spouse to a terminal illness. It felt to her as if she had lost Alex to death. He was gone from her life. How many times had she dreamed he would be killed in prison? Or that incarceration would change him, and he would turn his back on her once he got out?

All things pass, though, even the devastation of loneliness. Eventually, she emerged from her inner darkness— still heartbroken but at least able to find comfort in the peaceful silence of her empty home. Now that silence was gone. Interrupted by a return she had prayed would happen for many long hours and days and weeks. So why did it all feel so odd and unsettling?

Just give it time, Sylvia told herself, removing a bottle of chardonnay from the small cooler next to the pantry. *He's back home. Life can be normal again.* The way it used to be. The way it's supposed to be after seven lonely, tear-soaked years. Two thousand, five hundred, and fifty-five days. An eternity in her heart. *God willing, nothing will take him from me again.*

She filled a glass with wine and sipped it as she dished

her salad onto one plate and put Alex's sandwich on another. When he stepped up behind her and put his arms around her waist, she flinched and let out a tiny gasp.

Alex laughed and kissed her neck. "What's got you so jumpy?" he asked. His lips, wet from the vodka tonic, were cold on her skin. She turned and let him kiss her fully on the mouth as she pressed against him, enjoying the feel of his body against hers, the taste of the drink on his tongue, the tangy smell of his sweat, the pressure of his strong arms wrapping around her—all the things she'd missed.

"I just can't believe you're home," she said. "Back where you belong."

"Damn right, it's where I belong." He kissed her again, more intensely this time, then carried his glass to the freezer and took out a bottle of Absolut. He splashed some into his glass, added ice, poured in tonic from a plastic bottle on the island, and swirled it all around with his finger. "Did they remember to put in extra Russian dressing?" he asked, nodding at the sandwich on the plate.

"I reminded them twice."

"Good girl." He took a drink. "You have no idea how much I've missed this."

But she did, and she knew it couldn't be nearly as much as she had missed him.

"Every single bit of it," he went on. "The taste of your lips. The smell of your hair. The feel of this house. The buzz from a vodka tonic. I took it all for granted, baby, but no more. I'll devote myself to you now."

"Right," Sylvia said and giggled. "We'll live off love." While that sounded wonderful, she knew better.

"Don't worry. You won't have to worry about anything again."

"I hope not." She ran her fingers up his bare arm to show

she wasn't being harsh or nagging. "They're sure not taking you back on the force."

"You're right. I burned that bridge, and the bridge burned me." Alex laughed at his own cleverness. He always did. It used to annoy her. Tonight, she found it charming and wonderful. All the things she had grown to hate about him before prison she now believed she would love and cherish forever.

"So," she asked, "now what?"

"There's plenty of work in the private sector. Pay is way better too."

"Private sector. What does that mean, exactly?" She hoped it meant working for a security firm and not what she feared it meant.

He put his arms around Sylvia and pulled her close. "It means I love you. And you've got to trust me. I've got plans. Don't worry. We'll be fine. Nothing will mess us up again. I promise." And he kissed her.

TRANE WALKED ACROSS THE RECENTLY MOWED LAWN, STEPPED onto the small portico, and rang the doorbell. While he waited, he glanced up and down the street. Still quiet. Still peaceful. *God*, he thought, *how boring to live a suburban life. Practically sedentary. This is where you bring your dreams to die.*

He rang the bell again. When the door finally opened, Trane saw a leaner, more muscular Alex standing in the foyer, wearing sweats and a tight T-shirt.

"Hello Alex," Trane said.

"Jesus. What are you doing here?" Alex seemed more surprised than angry. "We've got no business left. All that shit died with prison."

"Hear me out. May I come in?"

"No, absolutely not. Sylvia's here and ... fuck. Why'd you come?" He looked over Trane's shoulder.

"I'm alone. I promise."

Still, the ex-cop hesitated.

"Have you been following the news?" Trane said. "It's just the beginning. Let me in. Please."

"Alex, who is it?" Sylvia called from the other room.

"Nothing to worry about," Alex shouted back. To Trane, he said, "Whatever you have to say, do it right here."

"I'm not going to talk to you about this in your doorway, for fuck's sake. Five minutes, that's all I need. After everything we've been through, don't I at least rate a cup of coffee?"

"Goddammit," Alex said. But he stepped back to allow Trane to enter.

"Thanks." As he moved past, Trane slipped his right hand into his jacket pocket.

Alex turned his back on him as he closed and locked the door. This allowed Trane a moment to swing around and lift the Taser he had removed and press it against Alex's neck. The cop shuddered and choked, dropping to his knees. Trane easily pushed him over onto his side and then kicked him in the head, hard enough to knock him unconscious.

WHEN ALEX CAME TO, HE WAS BACK IN THE FAMILY ROOM, sitting on a bar stool in the center. It took a moment for his eyes to clear, for everything to come into view. The TV screen held the paused image of the film they'd been watching—one of those big-budget, comic-book-hero blockbusters he had missed seeing while in prison. Their half-eaten dinner was still on plates on the coffee table in front of the brown leather sofa. Sylvia sat on another stool by the wet bar, the look in her eyes teetering between confusion and panic. Trane stood beside her, his gloved hand placed firmly on her shoulder.

Alex tried to get up off the stool. Only then did he realize that his hands and ankles were zip-tied to the stool. "What the fuck?"

"Easy," Trane said. "I need you to control that temper of yours. You still have one, right? Or did prison knock it out of you?"

"Alex, what's going on?" Sylvia asked, her voice quivering.

"It's okay, babe," Alex said. "He's just making a point."

"No," Trane said. "*This* is making a point." He grabbed Sylvia's left arm and twisted it back in one quick, brutal move. Bone snapped, and Sylvia screamed. "Now," Trane said to Alex, "let's talk."

4

Out at the picnic table, we dined on grilled red snapper with jasmine rice and steamed broccoli. Charley and I shared a bottle of pinot grigio, while Kathy stuck with ice water. It was a cool evening after the hot day, and the night sky was clear. A breeze brought the smell of honeysuckle into the yard. Lights from oil rigs sparkled in the darkness of Santa Barbara Bay.

"You okay, Katbird?" I said, glancing over at my daughter, watching as she pushed her food around on her plate the way she had done when she was seven years old. She looked up at me, the faintest trace of a welcome smile on her lips, one I hadn't seen in a while.

"You haven't called me that in years," she said.

"I know. Funny, huh? It slipped out. The most natural thing. Does it bother you?"

"No, I like it. I've missed it. And I'm fine, just not that hungry. I mean it's good and all. Thank you, Dad. But I'm a little tired from the shopping and walking around and stuff."

"Did you guys have fun in town?"

Kathy looked over at Charley. "Yeah, it was a good day." Her smile widened.

"It was, indeed," Charley said.

"I'm glad," I said.

"But I'm beat," Kathy said. "Is it okay if I clear my place and go to my room?"

"Sure."

She stood and kissed my cheek, then gave Charley a hug. "I really had fun," she said.

"Me too," Charley said. Kathy picked up her plate and water glass and went inside.

"Anything happen while the two of you were together?" I asked.

"No, she was doing okay," Charley said. "We shopped, got iced lattes, sat on the beach, and watched the sailboats and the kites. It was a nice afternoon."

"Did she talk about anything specific?"

"Not really. Mainly she humored my dumb attempts at triviality, and I didn't want to push."

"No, of course not." I frowned, disappointed, as always hoping that a little window into Kathy's psyche might suddenly open and allow us to help her. During the first month at the cabin, she had been silent and aloof, emerging from her room only when there was a meal to eat, or she had to use the bathroom. By the fifth week, she had started walking around the property and sitting with us on the front porch in the evenings after dinner. Only in the last few days had she participated in our conversations. Today's trip into town marked a big step for her.

Healing was a slow process, I knew, especially healing from a violent attack. Before coming to Santa Barbara, we had urged her to seek rape counseling. Kathy had refused— rather adamantly. She wasn't ready to talk about what had happened with anyone. *Least of all a stranger*, she said. Even if that stranger was a professional armed with the proper tools to teach her to cope with the trauma. I couldn't force her to do something she wasn't ready for. I could only wait it out and gently nudge whenever I thought it appropriate.

"Give her time, Jagger," Charley said. "This will be a slow process."

"I just wish she'd agree to see someone."

"Then we shouldn't have dragged her out of LA."

"I couldn't force her to stay either," I said. "She seemed to want to come up here as much as I wanted to bring her. Plus, I thought it'd be a week or two, tops. It's going on two months, and I still can't convince her to go back home."

"Maybe she's ready but is afraid to tell you."

"You think so?" I said.

"I'm just guessing here, but lately, I get a kind of sense she wants to go. She's just afraid to admit it. Or scared she's not as ready as she thinks. She told me today she missed her friends Claire and Debby. It's the first time she's even mentioned them."

"That's a good sign, yes?"

"It's something." Charley looked up at the moon, high above the trees surrounding the yard. It gave a surreal sheen to the land and cast a glistening, flickering line of white across the dark ocean below. "Or maybe she thinks you're afraid to take her home."

"Have I been hovering?"

"Sort of." Charley poured me some wine. Her glass was still nearly full. "You've got to admit you've been extra careful around her. And that's expected."

"Is it?" I said. "I don't know. I'm making this up as I go along."

"We both are."

It was true. I felt lost—filled with nervous confusion, the feeling you get when you turn a corner and found yourself in a seedy, unknown part of town. "It's an uncomfortable thing."

"It's not just because of what happened to her," Charley said. "It's also about what happened to you."

"My problems don't matter."

"And you've made that clear to her. It doesn't mean she believes you. She's smarter than that. So am I." Charley paused, studying me. "Something happened today, didn't it? With you?"

"Why do you think that?"

"Tire tracks on the gravel, not from your Jeep. Two whiskey glasses by the sink. And that troubled look you've had in your eyes since we got home."

I sat back and sighed. Charley was always good with details. It's what made her such a good cop. And I realized it was foolish not to share things. We were together again, in all senses. There shouldn't be any secrets.

"Hold on," I said, and went inside.

We settled on the front porch steps where we could get more of the nice breeze from the ocean. I opened the manila envelope and took out the documents and photographs Ellison had left for me. "All the evidence and background indicate the Horton family had no idea what the killer or killers wanted," I said and handed the crime scene photos to Charley. "They were just living in the wrong place."

"So whatever they were looking for must connect to you or Scotty."

"Or they think it connects to us." While she glanced at the pictures, I grabbed a rock from under my shoe and tossed it across the driveway. The forlorn call of an owl filled the silence. "It'd be foolish to think my old man never skimmed money from busts and stuff. He was in the thick of most operations, even as his crew's commanding officer. When you're undercover, it's easy to lose sight of the line. Hell, he stole that Alfa Spyder of mine, the one that got banged up in the crash back in February."

"I know how much you loved that car," Charley said. It had been a 1978 Alfa Romeo convertible, red with a tan leather interior—now a heap of scrap metal in a junkyard, totaled when someone decided they didn't like my investigation into Caligula and ran me off Malibu Canyon Road.

"I loved it because it came from my dad on my seventeenth birthday. I never cared that he took it from a drug dealer he'd busted, or a friend of his at DMV illegally switched the title over to my name. It was a present. I didn't ask questions. Who would?"

"It was a sweet ride. Dangerous and falling apart, but sweet. To be honest, I'm glad it's gone."

"That's not the point."

"No shit, Sherlock." She put her hand on top of mine.

"I knew the deal even then," I said. "And I doubt it was the only time my dad manipulated the law to his benefit. Look at the house we lived in. West Hollywood? Prewar? On a vice cop's salary? And he sunk a lot of money into making this cabin livable. All the guys in his crew lived well above their means. Paula Ramirez in Studio City. Alex Davis in Calabasas. Colin Parker's place was above the Sunset Strip, for Christ's sake." I picked up another rock and threw it after the first one, harder this time. It ricocheted off the gravel before coming to a stop at the edge of the grass. "I don't doubt that Dad played in the dirt sometimes. I'm sure he took a taste whenever he could."

"Given this," Charley said, pointing at the folder on the

step between us, "you've got to prepare yourself for the possibility it was more than just a taste."

"Do I?" I sat forward, resting my elbows on my knees.

"The house was the target," she said. "They dug up the backyard. They tore up the floorboards. They were looking for something specific. Something the killer would butcher a family to find."

"I know. And if rumors about Petrov's missing money are true, it makes sense that people would suspect Dad held onto it while the others were in jail. I get that. The Laurel Avenue house would be the first place I'd go if I were looking. But this is all supposition. There was absolutely no evidence tying my father to anything during the trial. Why would his crew take the rap, seven long years, and not drag my father along if he was guilty?"

"I can't answer that," Charley said. "But I can say one thing: this will not go away. Stuff may come out. You've got to be ready. And it'll torture you until you find out for sure."

"No," I said. "Even if it is true, nothing changes. I'm not getting pulled back in."

"Okay," she said, but I could tell she didn't believe me.

I wasn't sure I believed it myself.

fter cleaning up the dinner plates, we read in the living room for a while, then went to bed around eleven-thirty. While Charley slept beside me, I lay awake in a house as silent as an empty church. It still felt odd to share a bed—and a life—with her after so many years apart. Love is as perplexing and fickle as they say. Our relationship had disintegrated years before when she left the sheriff's department. We reconnected as friends during an investigation into the murder of a rock singer named Nora Lord and stayed in contact after. Things progressed. The friendship turned amorous again. The reunion took us by surprise. But something about being back together felt more right than wrong, at least to me. I wanted to believe that we had learned from our mistakes, and this go-round would last.

Around midnight, when I was still awake, with no sense that sleep would come soon, my thoughts turned darker and more disturbing. Ellison's visit had triggered in me memories of my father, of the man he had been: strict, aloof, prone to alcoholism and bouts of anger when he drank, followed by long periods of moroseness. Those memories, along with confusion about my place in the world, had me feeling anxious and confused.

His suicide still haunted me, as vivid in my mind after six years as the events of yesterday. I had found him slumped over at the kitchen table of the Laurel Avenue house, his gun on the floor by his dangling hand, a pool of blood forming a perfect circle around his head. He'd left a note: *I'm ready to go, Son. I've seen enough. I love you, and I'm proud of you. Pops.*

I had always believed his parting words were meant as a blanket comment on the life he had led as a vice cop. But had they held a more immediate and specific significance? Something that stemmed from feelings of betrayal at learning he ran a corrupt team? Or was it a clue to his guilt? A confession? Had he avoided their fate not out of innocence but cleverness? Did his suicide note refer to some part of a puzzle I didn't know about?

I hated myself for asking these questions and silently cursed Ellison for bringing this to my door. It was easy to refuse to get involved but harder to deny the doubts it all raised.

Under the weight of so much thought, exhaustion finally overtook me, and I dozed for a time. When I awoke some hours later, I felt hot and sweaty. I grabbed several tissues from the bedside table and wiped my face. My pulse raced from a dream I couldn't quite remember. I got up and splashed myself with cold water from the bathroom sink. Coming back into the bedroom, I noticed that Charley's side of the bed was empty.

I found her sitting on the living room floor, a lamp turned on beside her. She had spread the contents of Ellison's envelope out on the coffee table and held a page in her hand.

"Hey," I said from the other side of the room.

She let out a small yelp, looking up from the document, startled. "Jagger! Dammit. Don't do that!"

"Sorry," I said. "How long have you been out here?"

"I don't know. Awhile. I woke up and couldn't get back to sleep."

"So you came to snoop."

"Pretty much. What's your excuse?"

I sat down beside her and said, "I had a dream." As I told her this, it came back into focus, clear and in technicolor. "About my father. He was playing a saxophone, some jazz piece, loudly and poorly. We were walking through an alleyway. I told him to stop, yelling at him that he sounded horrible. He laughed and kept on playing. Then he disappeared around a corner, and I woke up."

"You don't need Freud to interpret that one."

"There isn't an interpretation," I said. "It's meaningless."

"Well, this isn't." Charley held up the document. "Did you notice that the front door of the Laurel Avenue house was unlocked?"

"I didn't notice anything because I haven't looked at any of it, except the photos Ellison showed me."

"Well, it was," she said. "There was a gate that led to the dog run, with a big padlock."

"I know. I lived there, remember?"

"According to the police report, the padlock wasn't cut or tampered with. The patio door was locked from inside. No sign of forced entry anywhere. Just the open front door. What does that indicate?"

"That the Hortons trusted the assailant enough to let him or her into the house."

"Kind of rules out Yuri Petrov, wouldn't you think?"

"Or any of his goons."

"Who can most easily gain the trust of strangers?"

"Cops," I said.

"Right. The next question is, why now?"

"You're thinking it's one of my father's old gang, fresh out of prison."

"Let's talk it through," Charley said. "One of them shows up at the front door pretending they're still on the job and connives their way into the house."

I played along, telling myself I was simply humoring her. "*We have reason to believe, blah, blah, blah … Danger to your family … Can we come in and check that everything's okay?*"

"A couple with a little girl in the house doesn't want to take any chances. Of course, they're going to say yes."

"And the killer's inside."

"Looking for five million dollars. Yuri Petrov's money that the killer thinks Scotty stole. They don't find it at the Laurel location so they moved on to the next of the crew on the list."

"Colin Parker. Which blows any theory about my dad's involvement."

"Unless he didn't hide the money at home. I mean, seriously, would you? Scotty might have made arrangements with one of the others before they went to jail. Or when he decided to kill himself, he told one of them where the money was. So now it's a process of elimination."

This new angle was troubling. I went over to the bar and poured myself a shot of bourbon. I asked if Charley wanted one. She shook her head.

"I haven't once heard you say my dad might not have been involved," I said.

"I'm playing devil's advocate," she said. "If he's clean, don't you want to know?"

"The sheriff's department has plenty of very capable homicide detectives who can figure it all out."

"Yeah, but they don't have the insight into this that you have. You knew these men and women. Plus, a family was murdered. That's got to be eating away at you. Not to mention the conflict it must bring up inside about your relationship with your dad."

I drank the shot, set the glass down, then turned, and stared at her. "Is that the only reason you want me to take this case?"

"I think you need to know the truth. What else?"

"You tell me."

Charley hesitated, then said, "I think I will have that drink." I poured her one and another for myself, then crossed back to the table. "Can I be honest?"

"Of course. Always."

"It's a stupid and selfish reason."

"I'll try not to hold that against you. Spit it out."

"First and foremost, I want you to take the case because I think you should for your own sanity."

"Okay. Now the other reason."

Charley crossed her legs in a lotus position. "I want you to go back to LA, so I get to go back too. Without feeling guilty for asking you or forcing you or making you feel you had to do it for me."

It was the last thing I expected to hear, and her words hit hard. "You're fed up with all this, aren't you? It's been too fast. Too soon. You're regretting it."

"Regretting what?"

"Us. Getting back together."

"No! God, that's not what I meant." Charley took hold of

my hand. "I don't regret this for a second. I'm talking about being up here. About not being in LA. I miss it. I miss home. I need the city, Jagger. I can only handle so much beauty and tranquility. I need some mess and noise and horrible traffic. I need junk food. I'd kill for an In and Out burger."

"Why haven't you said anything?"

"Because of how selfish it sounds. I hate myself for even telling you now. For even thinking it. I made the choice to come, to do this with you and Kathy. She's what matters most."

As if on cue, Kathy screamed in her bedroom, shattering the quiet of the night and cutting short the conversation.

6

Everyone cracks if you hit the right pressure points. It doesn't matter how tough one is or what vows one may have taken. They could have broken the law, done time, even killed people. All human beings—cops, priests, thugs—have a breaking point. Trane knew this.

Alex Davis was no exception to this rule. So when Trane fractured Sylvia's arm, snapping it back at the elbow, Alex's spirit died. His bravado drained away. As Sylvia's cries of pain turned to whimpers, Alex seemed to melt down into the stool as if he wanted to sink into the floor and disappear. As if he knew where all this was going.

"You didn't have to do that," he said, barely a whisper. "You didn't have to hurt her."

"But I did have to," Trane said. "You left me no choice. I had to make a point."

"You bastard ..."

"Where's the money?" Trane said, his voice as calm as a tourist asking for directions. "And where's the girl?"

"I don't know," Alex said.

"Don't you see how foolish it is to lie to me?"

"It's no lie!"

Trane took hold of Sylvia's good hand and pulled three fingers back. More bones snapped. Sylvia wailed in pain. Her eyes rolled back into their sockets. She looked close to passing out.

Alex cried out, "Leave her alone!"

Trane leaned in so close he could smell the booze on the cop's breath. "Then tell me what I want to know."

"I can't. On the soul of my mother, I have no idea, I swear."

"God, you're a mess," Trane said, staring at what remained of a man he had once admired. Prison had weakened the detective, for sure. Turned him into a coward. The fragility he saw now repulsed Trane. "Last chance, old friend." He slipped a knife from his jacket pocket and flicked out the blade.

"I was never your friend," Alex said. "Just … let her go. She's got nothing to do with this."

"That's the first true thing you've said tonight," Trane said. "Which makes it all the more heartbreaking."

Trane turned to Sylvia then and, with one powerful stroke, sliced open her throat. Blood splattered out like paint flicked from a thick brush.

"Oh, God!" Alex bellowed. "Oh, Jesus. You motherfucker!" Spittle flew from his mouth. His face turned as red as his wife's blood as he screamed.

Trane stooped down to look into the broken man's eyes. "One knows nothing about anyone until one knows everything. And now I know everything about you."

Trane jammed the knife into Alex's throat, the blade pushing deep into the jugular. The geyser of blood was thicker and more concentrated than had spewed out of Sylvia's neck, but Trane didn't mind it spattering his face. Its warmth felt invigorating. He stayed still, holding the knife in place, catching the last bit of life in his victim's eyes before it faded forever.

After searching the house, garage, and backyard, Trane sat behind the wheel of his car, listening to Roy Hargrove on the radio—a delicate version of the standard "What's New?" —while he watched the fire consume the Davis house. The flames were such a beautiful thing to him. Dazzling and brilliant, so full of power and destruction. When the front windows of the house exploded, Trane felt a chill run from his shoulders down into his hands. He stared at the growing blaze until the song ended, and he heard the fire engines, then he drove away.

In the safe darkness of his Studio City apartment, Trane poured two fingers of single malt. Joshua Redman's "Lush Life" played, while Trane looked down at the neon and phosphorescent glow of the nearby bars and stores along Moorpark. He sized up his situation.

Scotty would have gone to great lengths to protect what he cared about—the money, the girl. Someone else, a member of Scotty's old team, *had* to know something. Trane would be methodical. He would continue to work patiently, eliminating one after the other until he found the person who could tell him what he wanted to know. If Armando and Paula let him down, he would be left with a final option. Trane hoped it wouldn't come to that. Bracing dirty cops was easy. He knew their strengths and weaknesses, and he was infinitely smarter. But dealing with Jason Chance? That'd be a whole other pint of poison. One he didn't want to choke down unless absolutely necessary.

7

We brought the shaken Kathy into the kitchen. Her skin was pale, her hair matted with sweat, her breath short and sporadic. Charley turned on the lights and filled a glass with water from the sink faucet. I could see fear in Kathy's eyes, but she tried to downplay the whole thing, telling us both it was no big deal.

"Just a stupid nightmare," she said. Yet her hands trembled as she took the water glass from Charley.

"It's okay to still be scared," I told her. "And to feel confused and lost. The counselor at the hospital said this would take time. But you don't have to carry this pain on your own. It's a sign of strength, not weakness, to want to get help. Charley and I will do whatever is necessary to help you get it. However and wherever you want." I paused and then added, "Maybe this idea of serene isolation has run its course."

"Are you saying we should go home?" Kathy asked.

"Only if you want to."

"I thought you needed to be up here for your own

reasons. I don't want to make you go back just because of me."

"Forget about my reasons," I said. "Yeah, I thought getting out of LA might be a good thing for both of us, and it has been, for a while. But I'm wondering if perhaps we've stayed too long. There's only so much hiding out we can handle, right? Maybe it's time we both faced things, head on." A glimmer of what I could only interpret as hope flickered in her eyes. "We can go back," I said, "and we'll find somebody you feel comfortable talking to, about anything or everything. We'll take this all a step at a time. Does that sound okay?"

Kathy nodded, biting down on her bottom lip. "I'm ready if you are," she said. "Maybe it is time."

"We can leave tomorrow," I said.

Kathy smiled and threw her arms around me. She held me like she was afraid I'd suddenly disappear.

WITH LITTLE CHANCE OF GETTING BACK TO SLEEP, WE MADE pancakes, heated up slices of ham, doused it all with maple syrup, and then plopped down in front of the TV to watch *The Maltese Falcon*. Charley and I sat side by side on the sofa. Kathy took a spot on the floor between us, her back pressed against our legs. No one spoke, but I could feel warmth and unity, a sense of family, as if the decision to leave had brought us closer together.

When the movie ended, we picked up our plates, washed them in the kitchen together, and headed off to bed. At Kathy's request, I stayed with her in her room as she drifted off to sleep. I did this often when she was a little girl because of a nightmare or a cold she was fighting or for no other reason than she had trouble getting to sleep and

wanted me near. Looking down at my daughter now, I
longed for those days of normal childhood afflictions and
fears. The desire for a more innocent time was comforting
but foolish, I knew. We can't remain innocent and untainted
any more than we can stay young. We can only find strength
wherever possible as we move forward through *this thing
called life*, as the singer Prince referred to the craziness of
living.

I raised Kathy on my own practically from her birth. Her
mother was too young to handle the responsibility, so she
bailed on us and moved to New York when Kathy was barely
two months old. We hadn't seen or heard from her since.
When Kathy turned 16, I asked if she wanted to try to track
her mother down. She declined. *You're the only parent I need*,
she told me. I clung to that sentiment. Most of the time, I
believed I was all she needed as a parent. But I also thanked
God we had Charley in our lives. She became the mother
Kathy's biological one felt she could never be. And she gave
Kathy the strength to face these recent events in ways I
never could.

Once Kathy was asleep, I went to our bedroom, climbed
under the covers, and put my arms around Charley. We
kissed, cuddled, and closed our eyes. My last thought as I
drifted off to sleep was a moment I remembered witnessing
between Kathy and my father. She had found him drunk,
passed out on an armchair in the living room of the Laurel
Avenue house. She tried to wake him to get him to go to bed.
He opened his eyes, startled and scared, looking around like
he was in danger while cursing with drunken shameless-
ness. Kathy was only twelve at the time, but she never
flinched. Instead, she calmed him down, walked him to his
bedroom, and helped him get under the covers. I watched
from the doorway, not making my presence known, as he

touched her cheek and said, "You'll always be stronger than the lot of us, kiddo. Never let anybody take that away from you."

It was the best advice I ever heard my father give anyone.

WHEN I WOKE AROUND ELEVEN, CHARLEY WAS UP, MAKING coffee. Kathy sauntered into the kitchen just past noon, red-eyed and yawning. Nothing had changed for her with the sunlight of a new day. She was as determined this morning to go back home as she had been in the dark of the night.

We ate a light second breakfast of yogurt and power bars, then spent the next two hours packing our bags and loading them into the two cars, Charley's Prius and my Jeep Wrangler. Just after three, the housekeeper Evelyn Marbut arrived after I made a call to her.

Evelyn had been taking care of the cabin for the past fifteen years. Per my dad's request and his will, she had stayed on after he died, receiving a monthly stipend out of a joint bank account Scotty and I had set up. Her job was to come in once a week and check on the property.

In her mid-fifties, with full, dark hair just turning gray, Evelyn had what seemed to be a perpetually sad expression on her face, mostly in the eyes. I didn't know her well, didn't know much about where she came from or anything about her connection to my dad, only that he trusted her. I had always suspected there was some kind of history between them, but I never felt it was my place to press for an answer. I did as I promised—paying her weekly salary with money from my father's life insurance deposited into the account—and she did her job—working efficiently, without comment or conflict.

I told her we were leaving. Evelyn wished us well and

stayed behind to close up the cabin. I should have read more into the look of relief I saw on her face as we said goodbye.

We hit only a few pockets of mid-afternoon traffic going south and were back in Valley Village by 4 p.m. The house was stuffy and sweltering. Charley and I opened the windows and cranked on the air conditioning. Kathy grabbed only her things from the car and headed straight for her room. Not long after, I heard the pings of her cell phone and laptop computer. A good sign—it meant she was back to communicating with her friends. I didn't know which of them she had told about her ordeal—that wasn't my business—but at least she was reaching out, emerging from the cocoon she built around herself these past months. It was confirmation we did the right thing by returning to Los Angeles.

Charley was also relieved and energized to be home. Thirty minutes after we returned, she said she needed to get out and go for a drive, and she wanted to go alone.

"I need to get the city back in my blood flow," she said. She also wanted to check on her apartment in West Hollywood. We kissed, and she hurried off, leaving me with a pang of guilt at having kept her away from her beloved city so long.

A pyramid of newspapers stood stacked up beside the front door—I had put a hold on the mail but forgot to stop delivery of the *LA Times* before we left—and it took four armloads to get them into the house. I dumped all but the most recent two weeks' worth into the recycling bin out back. Kathy stayed behind closed doors, but I could hear her soft voice and gentle laughter as she talked to friends, so I left her alone and went into my study. I turned off the lights, closed the blinds, kicked off my shoes, and did a twenty-minute meditation session—a practice I had started doing before the Caligula case and tried to maintain with regularity ever since. I'd gotten off track while up in Goleta. Missing some of my twice-a-day sessions no doubt accounted for much of my disconcerted state.

Afterward, feeling refreshed, I made coffee and went out onto the porch with the most recent newspapers, along with the file from Ellison. Unable to stop myself, I scoured the periodicals, scanning headlines for anything pertaining to the killing of the Hortons and Colin Parker. The murders got some initial coverage but not a lot of follow-up. Homicides were abundant in the City of Angels, and the *LA Times* only had room for the most current and sensational.

In a recent edition, I found an article about the deaths of former vice squad detective Alex Davis and his wife, Sylvia. Like Parker, Alex had been a part of my dad's unit and served prison time. He and his wife had been murdered in their home. Like the Horton family, their throats had been slit, and the house set on fire.

I called Captain Ellison.

8

Trane drove down a ramp deep into an underground parking structure, descending three floors before he found a level with no other cars. He left the motor running and the radio on, trying to draw energy from Wayne Shorter's "Speak No Evil" as it played. He was tired. He wanted this all to be over. He longed for a time when he could close his eyes and not still see the blood of a day's work. He just needed to find the money and to find her. Then they would go away, disappear, head somewhere they could reinvent themselves. A place far away and safe.

A dirty, white van with no side windows pulled into a parking spot at the far end of the same row. The engine rumbled and belched smoke as a burly man in a weathered, leather jacket and black skullcap got out, walked around to the rear of the vehicle, and opened the double doors. He dragged out a skinny fellow wearing only white underwear briefs. His hands were zip-tied behind his back. Silver duct tape covered his mouth. The little man squirmed and whimpered as the bigger man dumped him on the asphalt.

With a nod at Trane, the driver climbed back into the

van and drove off, the van disappearing up the curving ramp. The garage smelled of garbage and gasoline as Trane walked toward the man on the ground, pulling on a pair of latex gloves.

"Hello, Darby," Trane said.

Blood covered Darby's cheeks and nostrils. His left eye had been beaten so severely it was swollen shut. He looked up at Trane with his good eye and tried to say something through the duct tape. Trane stooped down and yanked the tape off with a quick pull.

"Jesus!" Darby screamed. "What the fuck?" His good eye rolled around as if he might pass out.

"Stop it." Trane slapped him on the cheek. "Where are Armando Trujillo and Paula Ramirez? Where has Ellison taken them?"

"I don't ..." Darby tried to focus on Trane's face. "Oh God, I'm gonna throw up."

Trane slapped him again. "He put them in protective custody. I need to know where they are."

"Ellison's homicide, man," Darby said. "It's got nothing to do with me."

"One more chance." Trane took a knife from his boot and flicked it open. "Tell me where they are, and I'll kill you quickly. If you don't give me what I want, I'll take my time, and you'll be begging me to end your pain."

9

I met with Ellison in Studio City, at Art's Deli, a favorite haunt of the movie and television industry people. I sat in a booth near the back, sipped coffee, and waited, thinking about my father, his team, and Yuri Petrov. Mostly, I thought about that poor, innocent family who had bought their first home, not ever imagining it would be their last. My reticence to step back into the world from which I'd taken a much-needed break competed with two driving factors: my curiosity to learn the extent of my father's involvement in his team's corruption and my desire to avenge the murder of the Hortons.

The captain looked tired and irritable as he slid into the booth bench across from me. "Sorry," he said. "The drive from MP was brutal." Monterey Park, the location of our homicide division, was southeast of downtown LA, a horrendous drive up the 101 at most times of the day but worse after 5 p.m. I'd expected Ellison to blow me off when I asked if he would come to the Valley to meet, figuring he would tell me to see him at his office in the morning if I needed a face to face. My reason was that I wanted to stay close to home and Kathy. To my surprise, Ellison agreed without hesitation to drive up.

The waitress, a middle-aged woman named Velma who had worked there since I was first in uniform, stepped up to the table and refilled my cup of coffee. She always had a smile that looked like the start of a day. "I'll have the same," Ellison told her. Once Velma had gone, he said, "When did you get back?"

"A couple of hours ago."

"And you called me as soon as you got in."

"I read about Alex Davis and his wife."

Ellison took a deep breath then exhaled like he was about to whistle. When Velma brought him his coffee, he drank a healthy portion of the hot black liquid. "I'm running on fumes here," he said. "We just picked up Paula Ramirez and Armando Trujillo and put them in protective custody."

"Good. Who's handling the investigation?" All three murder sites were in LA Sheriff's Department jurisdiction.

"Karl Unger," Ellison said. "You ever meet him?"

I shook my head. "Any good?"

"Time will tell. He's smart. Helped make the Ebersol case. Remember that?"

I did. Christine Ebersol was a third-year student at USC whose body was found in a garbage receptacle behind The Roxy on Sunset one Saturday night the previous fall. In a fiendish murder worthy of the Black Dahlia killer, she was disemboweled and washed clean, her blood drained, her head and all pubic hair shaved. Crude tattoos were post-mortem inked across her body with a ballpoint. Egyptian hieroglyphics.

"Unger was the one who got onto her professor," Ellison said. "He felt all the work—the cutting and shaving and draining and inking—was overkill. Someone wanting the murder to look like the work of a psychopath to send us in the wrong direction."

"Anybody who can disembowel a woman and cover her body with tats *is* a psychopath, Captain, even if he is trying to throw us off."

"No question. But this guy thought he was clever. Ebersol was a student at USC, had an affair with her teacher. Guess what department?"

"Egyptian history?"

"No. Literature. Nothing to do with Egypt. He failed her on a paper on *The Fountainhead*. She got angry over the grade and threatened to tell his wife they'd been screwing around if he didn't change it to at least a B."

"And the poor guy who's not a psychopath snapped."

"Big time. Went to town on her, I guess hoping to make it look like the beginning of a serial killing spree. Unger took a closer look at him, interviewed him a few times, rattled him. He screwed up his story from one interview to the next, and it was enough to get a search warrant. The nut took pictures of her body and kept them on his computer, if you can believe that." Ellison signaled Velma for a refill. "Anyway, Unger's got a future."

"That's good. You need strong detectives."

"Yeah, but he's still not you, Jason."

"I appreciate that."

Velma arrived to top off Ellison's cup. He stared down into the black liquid, looking bone tired. "I hate dirty cops. I won't deny that." He was back to talking about my father's crew. "But these guys, Parker and Davis, they served their time. They paid the price for breaking the law. They didn't deserve this."

"Whoever is responsible isn't worried about deserve," I

said. "He won't stop until he gets what he wants, or we catch him."

"Then help us do that."

I ignored the comment. "Has Trujillo or Ramirez given you anything useful?"

Ellison shook his head. "They're clamped up tight. Claim they know nothing about the killer, the money, or the drugs."

"They could be telling the truth."

"Wouldn't that suck. They're the only leads we've got."

"Something else bothers me," I said. "Why did Colin Parker take a bullet to the brain, while Alex, Sylvia, and the Hortons were killed with a knife?"

"I've thought about that," Ellison said. "Maybe Colin wasn't so easily subdued. He was a big guy, and he could've had a gun in his house. He got hold of it. They fought. The killer took it away from him and used it out of necessity."

"That's one possibility."

"The rest of the MO matches, Jay. It's the same guy."

"Yeah, I suppose it is. Someone looking for money that may or may not exist. Killing off my father's team one by one to find out."

I rubbed my face with my hands. Ellison and I had effortlessly fallen back into our usual pattern of investigative questioning. Unlike other times, though, the routine made me anxious, like I was somehow betraying my dad. *Thanks for the vote of confidence, kiddo. It's good to know I can still count on you to have my back.*

"I know this is difficult for you," Ellison said, always insightful. "And I appreciate you reaching out to me today."

"We're just two men, batting ideas around. Doesn't mean anything yet."

"What would it take?" he asked.

"More than this conversation."

"Do it unofficially then. Just lend us your expertise for a bit. You've a better shot at solving this than anyone I know." He lifted his cup with both hands and drank, staring at me across the rim. "It doesn't matter if your father was as dirty as David Mack or as clean as Dick Tracy. Either way, he's at the core of this, and you know it. If somebody's killing people because of him, don't you want to stop that?"

Ellison could be the most tactful human being on the planet when he wanted. He could also be as blunt as a son of a bitch.

"I need to look at the murder book," I said.

10

Driving home, listening to Aimee Mann sing "Stuck in the Past," I thought back over the days and weeks before my father killed himself. Armando Trujillo, Paula Ramirez, Alex Davis, and Colin Parker had been locked up for four months when my dad pulled the trigger. Over the course of those months, had he made a statement or an action that might shed light on this new case? He'd been despondent, for sure. I figured it grew out of being upset over what he saw as personal betrayal by his team and learning the depth and breadth of their criminality. How do you face something like that? If I learned tomorrow that Captain Ellison had blackmailed suspects and fabricated evidence over the course of his career, how would I react?

Every cop walks that fine line between duty and temptation. And many cops have, at one time or another, bent the rules to get results. I was no exception—up to a point. I'd never taken a bribe or extorted money, but I had covered up a crime while closing out the Caligula case. Was a single time any less corrupt than ten or a hundred? Where was the line? *Was* there one? Cops operated in a world driven by deceit, chicanery, violence, and psychosis. Our careers were based on trying to right those wrongs. It was fair to say the line could easily blur. And sometimes, the *end* really did justify the *means.*

Three days before he killed himself, the day Kathy left for a school trip that fortunately put her out of the house, my father met with his commanding officer, Captain Chris Teller. Dad and he spoke for several hours behind the closed door of Dad's study, finishing half a bottle of Jameson's in the process. Dad never told me what they had discussed.

Maybe it was time I found out.

WHEN I GOT TO THE HOUSE, I GRABBED MY LAPTOP AND A BEER from the fridge and went out on the back deck. It was a cool evening, the mist a fine gauze that diffused the light of my backyard lamps. In the house that abutted my property, my neighbor, Jonah Whitcomb, an elderly retired firefighter, had a ball game playing too loudly on his TV. The cicadas in the yard seemed to feel the need to compete, their clicking song rising up from the bushes in an attempt to overpower the announcer's calls.

I shut out the cacophony as best I could and searched online for Captain Christopher Teller. He had retired two years after my father's suicide. I called a friend in the narcotics bureau and got Teller's phone number. He answered after several rings, sounding gruff and old.

"Jeez Louise, I haven't thought about Scotty in years," he said after I told him who I was. "Helluva thing. I still can't believe it. You doing okay? I keep track of your cases. That last one, Caligula? Man, oh, man. One thing a cop can count on: there are sick fucks everywhere, and they never disappoint."

"You sound like you miss the job," I said.

"Every goddamned day." He cleared his throat. "I read Scotty's team's been released. That why you're calling?"

"Indirectly. I wanted to ask you about that meeting you had with my father a few nights before he killed himself."

Teller went quiet. I heard a chair squeak across a floor, then a huff as he sat down. "I don't remember too much about it," he said at last. "We went heavy on the Irish, as I recall."

"Maybe talking about it now will shake something loose. Do you have time tomorrow? I could come by."

"What's this about, Jason?"

"I have some questions; that's all. Personal more than anything else. I'd like to pick your brain if you've got time."

He chuckled. "I've got nothing but time. Well, not as much as I'd like, not anymore. It goes fast. You'll find out soon enough how much it sucks, getting old."

Teller gave me his address. It was close by in Sun Valley, a quick drive up the 170. We arranged to meet at eight the next morning. I thanked him and ended the call.

THE SHADES WERE DRAWN IN KATHY'S ROOM, AND THE LIGHTS off, the only illumination coming from the screen of the open laptop on the bed. Kathy lay on her stomach, ankles crossed in the air, elbows bent, her chin resting on her open palms, her face hauntingly beautiful in the blue glow.

"Got a minute?" I said from the doorway.

"Sure." She kept looking at her computer, scrolling through Pinterest pins. "Where's Charley?"

"Checking on her place, running errands." I sat on the

edge of the bed and nodded at the laptop. "Think you could turn that off for a minute?"

"Oh yeah, sorry." She closed the lid.

"How are you feeling," I asked, "now that you're home?"

"Better, I guess. It's only been a couple of hours."

"True."

Kathy forced a smile. "So much drama, and all you wanted to ask was how I'm doing?"

My grin was sincere. "That's part of it."

"Okay ..."

"I met with Captain Ellison a little while ago. There's a case he wants me to look into."

"Was it him who came to see you up at the cabin?"

"How'd you know anyone did?"

"Charley said you had a visitor but didn't want to talk about it."

"Yes, that was Captain Ellison."

"Does this mean you're going back to work?"

"I don't know, and not if it makes you uncomfortable."

"No! Why would it? I think work will be good for you." She hesitated before continuing. "Don't get all crazy when I say this, but you've kind of been a helicopter dad these past couple months. I get why, but it hasn't made things any easier for me. It'd be nice for you to focus on something else for a change and give me some room to breathe. Are you mad I'm saying this?"

"No, I'm delighted." It was the clearest sign yet my old Kathy was returning. The girl who spoke her mind and took no shit, who pushed me away whenever I got too close or annoyed her. "You should have said something before."

"Dad, don't be stupid. It's normal. And part of me likes the attention, even while the other part wants to scream at you and tell you to back off. Does that make sense?"

I smiled and ruffled her hair. "Perfectly."

"So what is this case? No, wait. Never mind. Reset. I don't think I want to know."

"Okay, understood."

She sat up and leaned back against the headboard. "I've got news too," she said. "I called that doctor." She pointed to a business card on her night stand. "The one you suggested."

"Anna Ryker?"

"Yeah, I made an appointment for Friday."

I smiled. "That's my gal."

"Initiative, right? One step at a time?"

"No matter how small. And this is a good one."

"It better be."

"You want Charley or me to go with you?"

"God, no. What did we just talk about?" Kathy rolled her eyes. "I've got to do this on my own."

"Anna's very good at what she does. She'll know how to guide you to a place where you can get past things and open up."

"I'm scared. A little."

"That's normal." I put my arms around her and kissed her cheek.

"Okay," Kathy said, and then paused. When she spoke again, her tone had grown more tentative. "Can I ask you something?"

"Of course. Anything."

"The guy who abducted me ..."

"JoJo Sellars."

"When you shot him, did he have a gun?"

"Yes, he did."

"Was he about to use it?"

"I think he would have if I'd given him the chance."

"So it was self-defense."

"I made a judgment call."

"Would you have shot him anyway? Even if he didn't have it?"

"The minute I saw you in the bedroom, I acted." A wave of nausea came on as I said this. The back of my neck grew clammy.

"Are you going to face any charges?"

"No, the department considers it a good kill. Not that there ever is such a thing."

Kathy unfolded her arms and placed her palms down on her thighs. "I think there is."

"Let's just say there are some that are less egregious than others." My mouth tasted of copper. I felt an icy tingle along my shoulders.

"Dad? Are you okay?"

"Yeah, Katbird. I am. I just don't like thinking about what happened to you."

"But you understand why I needed to know."

"Of course."

"And I'm glad he's dead. I'm glad you killed him. Otherwise, I don't think I could ever close my eyes again."

"We all learn to close our eyes again, honey. Every single one of us."

"Like you? Going back to work?"

I fought down the acrid bile rising into my throat. "Like you said, one step at a time."

"For sure."

"I love you, Katbird."

"Love you too."

IT WASN'T UNTIL I REACHED THE BATHROOM AND CLOSED THE

door that the panic attack came on. I tried to vomit but only accomplished dry heaves. I slammed the toilet lid closed, then sat down on it with my fist in my mouth and tears stinging my eyes. My whole body shook. I was so cold that it felt like I'd been caught naked in a storm.

The dam of deflection and suppression I constructed over the past two months finally cracked under the weight of my conflicted emotions, triggered by a simple question from my daughter. I sat there, shaking and crying, wanting to scream. I feared this might be the beginning of a nervous breakdown.

Keep it together, Jagger.

Mercifully, the ordeal ended as quickly as it began. The shaking, the tears, the instinct to wail at the top of my lungs all ceased, and a cathartic peace enveloped me, like a blanket thrown by some good soul over a freezing man in the storm. I stood and splashed my face with water, then stared in the mirror. Blood-red eyes and a slight chattering of my teeth were all that remained of the attack. The terror had abated, the breakdown averted.

Charley found me outside half an hour later, sitting on the deck, nursing a second beer, and listening to the *Sleep Well, Beast* album by the National.

"Don't take this the wrong way," she said, "but you look like shit."

"Have a seat," I said. "I'll tell you about it. Want a drink?"

She poured herself a chardonnay, then sat across from me on the patio.

"I had a panic attack," I said. "Can you believe it? I had to lock the bathroom door and jam my fist in my mouth, so Kathy wouldn't hear me. I wanted to scream and break things."

"Wow, what triggered it?"

"Kathy asked if I'd killed JoJo Sellars in self-defense."

"Which you did."

"His gun was down at his side. I shot him before he raised it."

"He would have if you'd given him the chance."

"We'll never know."

"Yes, we do. I do. You and Kathy are alive because that son of a bitch is dead." Charley put her arms around me and held me close. "I'm sorry I wasn't here for you when the attack came on."

"You are now." I held her close, needing her touch, her warmth.

She pressed her hand against my chest. "But you're okay. It's passed."

"Yes, for sure. It was cathartic, to be honest. That word always seemed so pompous to me, but now I understand its meaning."

"Cathartic is good." She kissed me, soft, warm, and long. I relished the feel of her body against mine.

11

Darby gave nothing useful, so true to his word, Trane killed him slowly. He sliced down the man's forearm, making a single, wide gash that would bleed out, and added several other smaller cuts across Darby's body, including carving symbols into the skin. There was no method or reason to Trane's actions; he simply amused himself while he watched Darby die. This was the first murder he had enjoyed in some time.

He had lost count of the number of men and women he had killed over the years. Twenty-five? Thirty? One for each year of his life? It was hard now to keep track of what had become a mundane part of doing business. In most cases, he no longer even considered it to be murder. It was simply part of the job. The price he needed to pay to walk the line between two worlds. There were moments, of course, when it still brought some pleasure—like today, with Darby. Other times, it bothered him. Like having to kill the little Horton girl. That was bad. He had even debated letting her live. But wouldn't that have been crueler? She would grow up with the horrible memory of the slaughter of her parents. It would haunt her. Fear, then hatred would probably drive her life. Better to end it all with one slash to the throat. A mercy killing, really. Barely any pain. She was better off. In his mind, most who die were.

Murder and death had always been a part of Trane's life. When he was fifteen, he saw his first man die: his own father, gunned down in front of him at a convenience store in East Hollywood. They had walked into a robbery in progress. His dad, a twenty-year deputy with the LA Sheriff's Department, was off duty at the time but had his department-issued handgun in a holster under his jacket. He never had the chance to take it out. The shooter killed him and ran.

Trane felt no sadness or shock but a rush, the kind he would later find out was like a hit of cocaine. Why shed a tear? He hated the old man. The fucker's death was a relief.

Cops came and asked Trane all kinds of questions. He lied about the description of the shooter. He also lied about the wallet he had stolen from his father right before they arrived, telling them the shooter lifted it before he ran off. Eventually, a patrol car took him home, where his mother beat him mercilessly, as if the old man's death were his fault.

Nine months later, Trane killed his first man, stabbing to death a crass, loudmouth drunk who had been sleeping with his mom. Trane despised the asshole, who beat her as often as he fucked her. One morning, when he saw a fresh and especially nasty bruise on her eye and a cut on her swollen lip, Trane waited until she left for work, then grabbed a large kitchen knife, and plunged it six times into the sleeping man's chest.

The blood was warm and luxurious as it splattered on his face and arms. The act made Trane feel godlike. Once he

washed the knife in the sink and cleaned away the crimson
goo from his skin, though, a sense of fear—of panic—overwhelmed him. He puked in the trashcan beside the bed,
then rushed into his own room and locked the door. He put
on a Coltrane tape (he had listened exclusively to jazz since
he was twelve), playing the music so loudly the sound was
distorted as it came out of the cheap speakers. Eventually,
the fear passed, and calm settled over Trane, allowing him
to think rationally and develop a plan.

He dismembered the body in the bathtub with the same
knife, cutting it into pieces as he had seen done (or at least,
implied) in several movies. He put the pieces in plastic bags
and loaded them into the back of the pickup truck his father
had driven, and his mother held onto after his death. He
divided the body parts across the city: an arm in Inglewood,
the torso in Westchester, a leg in East Los Angeles, the head
somewhere in the Hollywood Hills.

The body was never found. The murder never came
back to haunt him.

His mom died a year later, OD'ing on pills and choking
on her own vomit. Social Services placed Trane in a foster
home in Banning, with a strict Christian couple. He hated
them more than he hated his father, and on the morning of
October 26, his eighteenth birthday, he packed a small bag
with all his belongings, left the house in the predawn hours
without so much as a goodbye, and took the first bus back
to LA.

He knocked around the city for a few years, working odd
jobs: repairing cars, loading trucks at a furniture delivery
warehouse, doing maintenance work at an apartment
building in Sherman Oaks—all the while stashing money
away, building his savings. At night, he cruised the streets,
listening to jazz, sometimes hanging out in bars, drinking on

a fake ID, and trying to connect with those he liked to call the *shadow people*. The ones living on the other side of the law. Criminals and lowlifes who could teach him the ins and outs of a world that fascinated him. Not because he wanted to be like them. He wanted to punish them.

When he turned 21, he applied for the sheriff's department training program. They accepted him without incident. His background check came back clean. The fact that his father had been a deputy, killed in the line of duty (as the department said in the press release), helped. Trane was in excellent physical shape; his medical and psyche evaluations were stellar. He excelled at both the written and physical components of the training program.

Seven months later, he had a badge and a uniform. He worked the streets of the East Los Angeles division—some of the toughest neighborhoods in LA—putting in his time, learning the ropes, all the while keeping his eye on a specific goal, the dream: narcotics.

12

Ex-narcotics bureau Captain Chris Teller looked older than his 62 years. Though he had shaved that morning, and his receding hair had recently been trimmed in the back and over the ears, his skin sagged dramatically at the neck and jowls, and the wrinkles around his eyes and forehead were more pronounced than they should have been. Red veins spider-webbed across his nose, matching the bloodshot lines in his eyes.

Teller greeted me on the porch of a three-bedroom postwar ranch house on Tuxford Street in Sun Valley with a large, lush front lawn. His white T-shirt and khaki pants were clean and pressed, his work boots looking new.

"It's good to see you, Jason."

"Thanks for agreeing," I said, and followed him inside.

"Been thinking a lot about Scotty since your call," he said. "Memory's a funny thing." He didn't elaborate.

He led me into a neat, organized kitchen, not what I'd expected from a divorced ex-sheriff's captain. His wife of three decades left him, I learned, six months after he retired from the department.

"I guess I was suddenly hanging around more than she wanted," Teller joked. "You want some coffee?"

"Only if you're having."

"Always. Doc says I need to cut down. Makes me laugh. Like he's trying to keep me alive. I've got liver cancer. On my way out. But *cut down on coffee*, he tells me, because my BP's high. Doctors are funny people."

Teller took two mugs from a cabinet and filled both with coffee from a small, expensive-looking machine next to a newer-looking microwave oven. The floor and dinette table were clean. There were no dirty dishes in the sink or takeout food containers stacked up on the counters. The room smelled of lemon and disinfectant.

"Here you go," he said and handed me the mug. "Sugar's there on the dinette, and there's some two percent in the fridge."

"Black's fine."

He spooned some sugar into his mug. "You look good," he said. "I haven't seen you since the funeral. Hard to believe it's been six years."

"Coming up on seven."

"Jesus, time flies when you're dying." This brought another soft cackle.

"I appreciate you agreeing to talk with me," I said.

"*No problemo*. You want to sit in here or out back on the deck? Already feeling like it'll be a hot one, but it's prettier out there."

"This is fine, Chris, right here. I don't want to take up too much of your time."

"Like I said on the phone, I've got nothing but the little time I have left." Teller rubbed his hand across his smooth chin and cheeks. "I've been thinking about that night with Scotty. Trying to recall as much as I can. I remember he sounded troubled. Said he needed to get something off his chest."

"What was that?"

"I don't know. Never found out. At least I don't think I did. By the time I got there, he had already soaked up half that bottle of Jameson's, so he wasn't at his most coherent. Something was bothering him, I could tell that much, but we never ever got to the point of it. We were alone in the house. Kathy had gone out of town, and you were off working on something."

"The Ian Shrager case."

Teller nodded, tapping his index finger against his coffee mug. "Yeah, yeah, that was it. I remember because there'd been some crossover between you guys and us."

"Shrager worked for Yuri Petrov."

"Right, his bodyguard. Some diver found him under the Malibu Pier, right?"

I nodded. "Shackled to a piling. He'd been shot in the chest. The fish had gone to town on him."

"You ever clear it?"

"Nope, Ben and I never cracked that one."

"Ben Atkins. There's another name from the past. Another sad story."

"Yeah," I said. Ben had been my partner and friend for many years. His murder had launched the Caligula investigation. "Anyway, about that night with my dad ..."

"Well, he was already two sheets to the wind when I showed up. He did love the Irish, not that I didn't. So we sat in his study and drank whiskey and talked about old cases at first. You know, two soldiers sharing war wounds. I started thinking all Scotty wanted to get off his chest was the past. I know it hit him hard, learning what his team had been doing behind his back. That's not something you forget after a few months. Or years."

"Did you ever think maybe he was involved? You know, as guilty as they were."

"Ah, I get it now. That's why you're really here. Those punks are out and free. People are dying. You're worried there's a connection to Scotty. You want me to tell you your old man was a saint."

"Was he?"

"Of course not. No man is. Even the ones they made saints were just guys and gals who got lucky, people who did a few good things that made others take notice. But every man's got shit under his fingernails, Jason. You, me, the pope. We all fuck up at one time or another. It's what makes us human."

"Did my dad say anything that night about money that supposedly went missing from Yuri's compound?"

"The infamous five million dollars? He might have mentioned it."

"As in *I took it*? Or *I know who did*?"

"He asked what I thought might have happened to it. I told him I always suspected Parker."

"Colin Parker?"

Teller nodded. "Now there was a smart cop. Fearless motherfucker too. Forget the dirty part for a minute. Far as I know, he only ever stole from scumbags. I'm not condoning it, not for a second. But Parker got the job done. He brought Yuri down. There's something to be said for that."

"Sounds like you're sorry he got nailed."

"I'm always sorry to learn a cop messed up. From whatever. A brother goes down, a son, a father ... it's sad. We walk a fine line out there, Jason. Homicide's different, so you don't know. For those of us in narcotics, it's a fucking war zone, every second of every day. You want to talk about terrorists? The Yuris, the Chapos, and the Escobars of the world are as much national threats as all the killers out there trying to blow up our planes and shit."

"Did my dad agree? About Parker and the money?"

Teller shrugged. "All he said was whoever took it had to be careful about where they hid it because one day those motherfuckers would get out of prison, and they'd be looking for some security."

"Seems he was right."

"It was the kind of ballsy thing Parker would do. Plus, Parker was on the inside in the thick of Petrov's organization. Working undercover. He had the access."

"But he didn't have much time. They were all arrested within forty-eight hours of the raid on Petrov's place."

"Yeah, but Parker had months to plan. He could've gotten the cash and the drugs out before they even took Petrov down. It's not like he expected to get busted. Maybe he stashed it away somewhere, and somebody knows or suspects he did it. That's what the killer is looking for. They killed Parker. They killed that family. And they killed Alex and his wife. Could be you're looking for one of Petrov's men. Or someone else on Scotty's team."

"Only two possibilities left," I said.

"Trujillo and Ramirez. Unlikely on both counts. Trujillo's a coward. And Ramirez, well ... not to sound sexist, but she doesn't have the balls to murder six people."

"What if it's Yuri Petrov himself?"

"Fuck him. That bird's gone with the wind. He's a wanted felon. An escaped con. He's got cash spread out all across Europe. No way he's sticking around over five million dollars and a few keys of smack. Don't waste your time."

"Then there's nobody," I said.

"No, I guess not," Teller said, looking down at his hands. His fingers did a delicate tap dance across the tabletop.

"Unless my father took it," I said. "He had the opportunity. He was part of the raid, part of the arrest."

"I don't buy that," Teller said. "He takes five million, then kills himself? Just leaves the money out there somewhere? Never tells a soul?"

"Maybe he did tell someone." I let the statement hang.

Teller gave me a wry smile. "I'm not holding anything back, Jason. I've got no family, no one to whom I could leave something behind. And I'm no killer. I'm a dead man walking."

"Then I guess that rules you out."

"Sorry to disappoint," he said, laughing.

"Elimination is helpful."

"It sure is." He paused. "Scotty was always proud of you. You were the child he got right, he said."

"Easy to do, being as I'm the only one," I said.

"Yeah, there's that."

The silence that followed grew awkward, and I finally stood up. "I appreciate you taking this time, Chris."

"My pleasure." Teller also stood. "And listen, there are some people who think death forgives a lot of things. I'm one of them. Scotty made his share of mistakes. I've made mine. So have you."

"No question."

We shook hands at the front door, and I walked across the lawn to my car. I glanced back at the house one last time. Teller stood in the doorway, his arms crossed on his chest. Our discussion troubled me. Not because of what he said but because of what he hadn't. My father's old boss knew some secret. I could see it in his eyes.

13

"Jason Chance?" A man in a tweed blazer stood outside my front door. "I'm Karl Unger. Ellison filled me in. I've been dying to talk you." A thin sheen of sweat covered his forehead, and sweat stains splotched his white button-down shirt. His red and blue tie, loosened at the collar, clashed with the busy pattern of the jacket placed in the crook of his arm.

"The captain speaks highly of you," I said. shaking his hand. "Nice work with that Ebersol case."

"Thanks. It's all about observation. You're a legend in that respect. Nora Lord. Caligula. The Canyon Killer. The Evans murders. I bow to you, sir."

"Don't. It's like you said, all about observation. We just put the pieces together and hope they fit. Come on in."

I led Unger to the living room.

"Nice digs," he said, looking around slowly, carefully, as if taking in a new crime scene.

"Thanks," I said. "Did you bring the murder book?"

Unger smiled and smacked his messenger bag.

"Good," I said. "Let's get to work."

We sat on the deck with a pitcher of iced tea and Unger's book. Kathy had gone for a run around the neighborhood. I had asked Charley to join us—hoping for her input, wanting her to feel a part of things—but she bowed out, telling me she didn't want to be the *civilian* stepping on Unger's toes so early in the collaboration. I reminded her that I, too, was a *civilian* at this point. She headed off without further comment.

"Hey, tell me something," Unger said as he squeezed the juice from a lemon wedge into his tea. "Why do they call you Jagger?"

"Just a nickname. I love rock music."

"*Jagger.*" He smiled. "I'm not much of a Stones fan. I always loved U2."

"A very good band." I reached for the murder book to change the subject. "Did Colin Parker live alone?"

"Yep." Unger set his glass down and scooted his chair closer to mine, so he could look over my shoulder.

"No witnesses?" I turned to the first page of the chronology log.

"None so far."

"Who discovered the body?"

"Paramedics. A neighbor called in the blaze. By the time they got to the place, there was little of left of Parker that was recognizable."

"He'd been out of jail, what? Two weeks?"

"If that."

"No coroner's report yet?"

Unger shook his head. "But there was a clear gunshot to the back of his head. I doubt anything will come up to contradict that as cause of death."

"No knife wounds at all?"

"None," Unger said. "That's the one inconsistency with

the other killings. Everything else is the same. The victims tied up and murdered. The place torn apart and set on fire." Unger leaned back in his chair, stretching out his legs and crossing his ankles, settling in. "I'm intrigued by the theory of that missing money from Petrov's compound."

"We all are," I said. "It would be nice to have more proof of its existence. Any idea who put together the evidence against my dad's crew?"

"A task force cop named Eddie Gilmore," Unger said. "He was also working undercover in Petrov's organization, but he went in specifically targeting Parker. His mission was to get close to him, play him the way he was playing Petrov, and hopefully gather enough intel to bring warrants against your father's team. Parker was a smart cop. If he gave stuff up to Gilmore, he had to know what he was doing."

"You're thinking maybe there was some sort of collusion between them?" I asked.

"Go with me for a minute. Let's say Parker somehow gets on to Gilmore's true identity. He's already decided to steal Petrov's money and hide it away. Parker knows Gilmore is after the team, so they make a deal: 'Let me slide, and I'll split the five million dollars with you.'"

"Go on," I said. I knew where he was headed. I also saw the flaw.

"But Gilmore double-crosses him," Unger said. "Sends the whole crew to jail, Parker included. Gilmore probably tried right away to find the five million himself, but he couldn't figure out where Parker hid it, so Gilmore patiently waits seven years. Once the team is released from jail, he hits Parker, tries to pressure him into giving out the location of the cash."

"Except he didn't kill Parker first," I said. "He went after the Hortons. He could have done that six years ago. Why wait?"

"Shit," Unger said, looking disappointed. "Good point."

"I like the Gilmore angle, though," I said. "That there might have been some collusion with Parker. Where's Gilmore now?"

"Good question. I'll reach out to IA, get a contact for him." Unger glanced at his watch. "Meanwhile, we've put Trujillo and Ramirez into hiding. They both have strong alibis for all three attacks. Trujillo spent the weekend in a hotel in Laughlin with a woman he met playing Blackjack. We've got her name; we've talked to her, and there are a dozen dealers, bellboys, and bartenders who put them together at various locations throughout the hotel the whole time."

"What about Ramirez?"

"When the Hortons were killed, she was visiting her dad at a senior living facility in Indian Wells. In his room with him, watching TV. She stayed at a nearby Courtyard Marriott. A guy delivered a salad and a pizza to her thirty minutes before the one-hour murder window opens up for the Davis murders. Doubtful she could've gotten back to LA in time."

"Close to impossible," I said. "What about when Parker was killed?"

"She's got nothing for that one. Says she was in LA and home alone all night. But whoever did one, did them all, right?"

I agreed. We were looking for one killer. Someone after money or information that they believed my father's narcotics crew held.

"So what do you want to do next?" Unger asked.

"I'd like to interview Trujillo and Ramirez, but first I

want to walk the murder scenes. I need to see the places with my own eyes, take in the scenes with my own instincts working."

"I get that. Let's do it," Unger said as we both stood. "Listen, before we go, I need to get something straight with you, so there's no confusion later. Ellison says you're not back on active duty yet. You're still on leave from the department by your own choice. I welcome your consulting insight, but this is my case. I run the interviews. I call the shots. We clear on that?"

"The last thing I want to do is step on your toes, Karl, but I need to get something straight with you: I didn't ask for this. Ellison came to me. He thinks I can bring a perspective to things. I'm consulting at his request. Which means I'll go where my instincts take me, and I'll ask whatever questions I want of Trujillo, Paula Ramirez, and anyone else I deem appropriate. If I want to follow some lead on my own, I will. I'll keep you in the loop because that's the fair thing to do. And I have no intention of getting in your way, but I don't work for you. I'm not tagging along. If you have a problem with that, you'll need to take it up with the captain."

I watched Unger's face turn red. I wondered if he might punch me. To my surprise, he swallowed his pride and said, "I understand where you're coming from, Chance. Like I said, I welcome your insight. All I want to do is solve this."

"Me too. Let's go."

14

W
e took Unger's car and drove to West Hollywood, to Colin Parker's small, mid-century house on North Clark Street, above the Sunset Strip. Only a third of the front façade remained. Fire had obliterated most of the back wall, allowing us a view straight through to a deck that overlooked the LA basin. Ash and crumbled, black wood covered the floors inside. Soot caked what was left of the walls. The glass of the windows on each side of the building had blown out, leaving only charred frames. Most of the roof was caved in.

"Where'd they find his body?" I asked.

Unger led me to the bedroom and pointed to a blackened mattress. "Right there."

"Face up or face down?"

"Down. He was tied like this." Unger crossed his arms behind his back. "Same zip-ties as used on the Hortons." Another MO consistency.

"Single entry wound?"

"Yeah, pending autopsy. Like I told you, there wasn't much left of the body. A place this small goes up fast. The arson investigator believes the blaze began in here. Probably with the body."

I wondered again: why a gun and not a knife? It was the one anomaly. Ellison's explanation of a struggle didn't jibe with Unger's description of the killing, which seemed like an execution. The killer succeeded in subduing him, zip-tying his arms behind his back, then shot him in the head. Parker was alone in the house. The attack had happened in the early morning. The killer most likely surprised him in his sleep.

Maybe the later throat-slashing had been done to scare Abigail's parents and Alex Davis while they were still alive— a slow and gruesome action to force them to give up information.

"Why not come in to search when nobody's home?" I said. "Murdering a family of three is risky and difficult. Killing an experienced undercover cop even more so."

"Unless you're a psycho and enjoy it," Unger said. "And if you've got the element of surprise on your side …"

I walked through the rest of the house, looking at what-ever was still recognizable, hoping to get a glimpse inside Colin Parker's mind. Pockets of the structure were less destroyed than others. A poster of John Coltrane from a 1963 concert in San Francisco lay on the floor near the fireplace, only half-way burned. An extensive vinyl record collection on a shelf beneath the remains of a high-end stereo set was all but demolished, the covers blackened or completely obliterated, the vinyl warped or melted into black heaps. The titles I could make out were jazz recordings, mostly bebop. My dad and Parker had that in common.

"Did you bring in the murder book?" I said.

"It's in my bag in the car," Unger said.

"I'll get it."

I went outside, retrieved the book from Unger's satchel, and looked through the list of personal effects taken off the body at the morgue: a wallet, destroyed; a Rolex wristwatch; a St. Jude's medal on a chain around the neck; a skull ring; a silver earring in the form of the hand sign of the devil, with thumb and little finger extended. The last two were symbols of a more rock-and-roll attitude, which didn't coincide with the poster and album collection inside. Which could just mean Parker had eclectic tastes.

I tried to call up a mental image of the detective. Tall, muscular. Attractive in a rugged way. He was the youngest and the newest on the team when I met him. I was on to my own life by then, so he was an enigma to me, my memory of him the vaguest.

"What are you looking for?" Unger asked, coming out the front door.

"Just trying to get a glimpse inside the man."

I looked at photos in the book of Colin Parker's burned body. There was something about the way the shoulders slanted down that caught my eye. What I could remember of Parker was a bulky, imposing figure. But memory is a funny thing. Maybe his commanding attitude made him only seem bigger and scarier.

"We should head out," Unger said, "if we're going to check out the other sites before we meet with Trujillo."

I scanned the burned-out house one last time, then we took off.

Next stop, Laurel Avenue.

I hadn't been inside the house where I was born for six years, not since selling it to the Hortons, though I had occasionally driven past. On those rare times, I felt little more than nostalgia, my affection for the place dying with my father. Over the years, I developed a much stronger attachment to our property in Valley Village. So it surprised me that a lump rose in my throat, and tears stung my eyes as we approached the charred remains of the home.

"You sure this won't be too much?" Unger said as we got out of the car.

I had no answer for him, no idea how I felt walking in after so much time and emotional distance. I had spent six years laying to rest the sins of my father as I knew them. Now, I had decided to dig into the past in search of others I only suspected. I would have to look into Scotty Chance's soul from a new angle. I knew I might see things I wasn't ready to face, learn things I might not want to accept. Time heals when you allow yourself to let go. Memory and discovery are antithetical to that process. Looking back on the past might be like ripping the scab off a wound.

That someone slaughtered an innocent family here, possibly because of things my father did or knew, added to my anxiety.

But I told Unger I'd be fine and headed for the front door.

The walkway and steps were littered with cigarette butts too clean and fresh-looking to be more than a few days old, left most likely by the recent cops and detectives on the scene. Police tape stretched across the square posts of the porch. Fire had destroyed most of the right side of the structure, eating through the living room and causing the floor of Kathy's upstairs bedroom to collapse. The left portion of the house had far less damage, though the front windows, upstairs and down, had been blown out, and the wood sills and front door were singed and crumbling.

Entering the house, a nasty stench of burnt wood, smoke, and destruction hit me, stronger than in Parker's place. The hardwood floors of the foyer had been ripped up from their anchoring. The oriental runners along the hallway and going up the stairs were reduced to gray dust. Little remained of the living room wall against which the killer had lined the Hortons up and cut their throats. Flames had eaten away the plasterboard, exposing blackened two-by-four studs and a tangle of twisted, melted electrical tubing.

I closed my eyes and tried to image the Hortons on their knees in front of the wall. Had he blindfolded them? Maybe the little girl. Not the parents. He'd want them to see so they'd be scared, horrified, and tell him what he wanted to know. He most likely slaughtered Abigail first. Then Jackie. Dale would've been last. The poor man, innocent and clueless, forced to watch his family die to get information he did not have and could not give.

"I'm going upstairs," I said.

"Careful," Unger said. "I don't know how safe it is."

"I'll stay to the left. That side's not as badly damaged."

"Suit yourself. I'll be here waiting when you're done."

Kathy's bedroom and the second-floor bathroom were shells. I could see what was left of the living room through holes in her floor. In eerie contrast, the opposite side of the house seemed almost intact. The walls and closed doors were darkened with smoke but looked sturdy. The hinges of the door to my old room creaked as I pushed it open and stepped in. The Hortons had turned the bedroom into a home office. As a child, I had adorned my walls with Star Wars and Batman posters. In my teen years, the posters changed to rock bands—The Psychedelic Furs, The Cure, U2, David Bowie. Now, the walls held black-and-white photographs of New York, Paris, and Monte Carlo. A mahogany desk was by the window, perpendicular to a loveseat and end tables of espresso-colored wood supporting teardrop-shaped, dark-green ceramic lamps.

The room was a mess but not from the fire. The place had been vandalized. The contents of the desk drawers and end tables were scattered across the floor. The loveseat cushions were thrown on the floor and ripped open. The intruder had slashed the back and bottom of the sofa with some sharp object. A bookcase lay overturned, books piled all around it. The closet interior had two file cabinets, opened and searched. Papers were strewn everywhere. The searcher had been careless and sloppy, probably figuring it didn't matter because he planned to burn down the home.

I moved on to my dad's bedroom, the next one down the hall. The corridor floorboards felt unstable under my feet, and for a moment, I feared I might plunge through. I had an image of falling into the kitchen, crashing down on the table, and breaking my back. Perhaps dying inches from the spot where my father had pulled that fateful trigger.

"How's it going, partner?" Unger called up.

"Fine," I said. "Being careful."

"Good," he called back. "Take your time," he added sarcastically. "I've got nothing pressing to do."

"Ten minutes, tops," I said.

I stepped into similar chaos in my father's room. Under a window overlooking the backyard, the seat and backing of a yellow, velour chaise lounge was shredded. The king-sized mattress, pushed off the bedsprings so that it hung halfway the frame, had a gaping gash down its middle. A 55-inch flat screen TV set lay overturned, shattered, and the vintage, brown traveling trunk that had supported it was wide open, its contents of linens and pillows pulled out and scattered everywhere.

In the closet, clothes lay on the floor in piles. Shoeboxes

were overturned, their receipts, unopened letters, and photographs dumped out. A trapdoor in the ceiling above was ajar, off its frame.

Nothing in the room was recognizable to me; little of my father's possessions remained. The only thing that looked familiar was the traveling trunk. I stepped closer to examine it. Initials were etched into the large, center clasp lock: *PTC*. Phyllis Teresa Chance. My grandmother, my father's mother. We had stored the large box in the attic, and I forgot to remove it when Kathy and I left the house. The Hortons must have assumed we didn't want the thing.

A collection of photo albums filled the trunk's bottom, with dates written on 3x5 cards attached to each cover. The albums contained pictures of typical family fare: vacations, playdates in the park, picnics on the beach. The Hortons seemed like a happy family. I took the albums out, one by one, and stacked them on the floor. With the trunk empty, one corner of the cardboard bottom now curled up slightly. I took hold of the edge and raised it up, revealing a shallow space beneath—a compartment about two inches deep, filled with journals with black-and-white covers, like those used by children in school. There were twenty of them, stacked two high, across the bottom. I picked one up, opened it, and immediately recognized the handwriting.

JUNE 16, 2010—SC PERSONAL FILES. NOT FOR OFFICIAL EYES.

We made the connect tonight. Eight months of undercover work paid off. The prize contact. Yuri Gregori Petrov.

I FELT A TINGLE IN MY CHEST. A QUICK PERUSAL OF TWO OTHER

randomly chosen notebooks confirmed—these were my father's journals.

I quickly searched the room again and found an empty blue backpack on a shelf in the closet. It proved the perfect carrier for the twenty journals. I filled its main pocket with them and then hid the backpack behind the chaise lounge. I didn't want to show anyone the notebooks until I had some time alone with them.

UNGER WAITED FOR ME IN THE KITCHEN.

"Find anything?" he asked as I entered.

I shook my head. "A waste of time." He asked if I still felt the need to see the Davis house. "No," I said. "There's nothing I can't get out of your murder book. It's quite thorough."

The compliment pleased him. "Good," he said. "We've got about an hour until we're scheduled to meet with Trujillo. Wanna grab a bite?"

It was the perfect opportunity to free myself up. I told him the visit to my old home had chased off any appetite. Instead, I wanted to walk around the neighborhood to clear my head. "I'll grab an Uber and meet you for the interview," I said.

Unger didn't argue. I sensed he wanted a break from me. He gave me the address where we were to meet, then jumped in his car and took off. I hurried back inside the house, retrieved the backpack with the journals, and then walked up to Santa Monica Boulevard in search of a dark, empty bar where I could sit in peace and read.

15

JUNE 19, 2010—SC PERSONAL FILES. NOT FOR OFFICIAL EYES.

He's a smart soldier, Parker is. Newest to our team but seems to fit in well. I like him. He's only been with us six months, but I can already tell he's got an excellent feel for undercover work. Captain Teller likes him too. There's an edge to the guy, a fearlessness. Ramirez gives him a hard time, but she's got an excellent feel for being a pain in the ass, so no surprise there. She's a good cop, but she doesn't like change. Can't trust new things, so Parker's arrival and attitude don't sit well with her. I'm not worried. Parker's tough enough to stand up for himself. Plus, he got us where we needed him to—inside Petrov's group—so we owe him some gratitude. Parker's gonna go places, for sure —if he doesn't burn out or turn rotten. I've seen both things happen to the best. And to the worst. Narcotics can be a fucked-up department. Takes a special kind of character. Not like working homicide, where death is death. In Jason's world, you come in after the fact. You analyze and draw conclusions. You solve the murder, or you don't. Not to take anything away from what my son does—it's just that our stuff is different. We're about getting inside the hurricane and hoping we can stay alive. Sometimes, the hurricane kills you. Sometimes, it turns you inside out, makes you into the very thing you're hunting. Takes a special kind of cop to survive. I hope Parker's up for that.

READING THIS PASSAGE, I WONDERED IF MY FATHER HAD already started to suspect his team might be dirty. *Turned inside out*, as he wrote.

JUNE 22, 2010—SC PERSONAL FILES. NOT FOR OFFICIAL EYES.

Parker's making progress. That means, so are we. Slow and steady. That's the motto. He seems to have gained almost everyone's trust in Petrov's inner circle. It's a mixed bag. So far, this one guy's been the only real problem, according to Parker. A young punk named Eddie Gilmore, who seems to want nothing more than to give Parker shit. Bullshit actions, childish even, probably done to test him. Parker says he's got him under control. Hope that's really the case.

JULY 16, 2010—SC PERSONAL FILES. NOT FOR OFFICIAL EYES.

Parker hasn't been able to find out what exactly Gilmore does for Petrov or where he is in the food chain. Muscle possibly, though Alex has never seen him carrying a piece. And he's a lightweight, Parker says. More brains than brawn. Easy to beat the crap out of, if it ever came to that. Parker thinks maybe he's some kind of advisor, even though he came in after Parker did. Whenever Petrov has a meeting behind closed doors, Gilmore's usually called in. I told Parker, "Get the guy to trust you. Don't rub him

the wrong way. If he's advising Petrov, he could be valuable."
Parker agrees, but there's danger in that. Nothing is more suspi-
cious than trying too hard to get on somebody's good side. Parker's
gonna have to go carefully—and above all else, watch his back.
This is too important to blow just because one guy couldn't be
won over.

AUGUST 22, 2010—SC PERSONAL FILES. NOT FOR OFFICIAL EYES.

Things almost went off the rails tonight, but Parker rolled
with the punches (literally) and came out okay. Here's how he
described what went down:

"Eddie Gilmore's Benz comes up alongside me, signals for me
to pull over. He's got Yuri and a guy named Ian Shrager in the
backseat. Shrager is Petrov's main bodyguard. I ease over to the
curb. Gilmore pulls to a stop in front of me. Shrager gets out and
comes over. 'What's up?' I say.

"'We'll see,' Shrager says, and motions for me to get out of the
car. I do. Suddenly, Shrager grabs me and drags me off toward a
dirt field on the side of the road. Meanwhile, Gilmore and Petrov
get out of the car. Gilmore's glaring at me like I'd called his mother
a whore or something. I know right away he's behind whatever is
about to go down.

"When we get to the middle of the field, Shrager turns me to
face him and slams his fist into my gut. I double over, staggering
back and coughing. The punch hurt like a motherfucker.

"Petrov and Gilmore come over then. Petrov's as cool as can
be. Except his eyes. I can see fire in them. Fury. And I'm thinking,
something's gone wrong. I'm fucked. When he gets close enough,
Petrov grabs my collar and pulls me up, so we're eye to eye. 'Eddie
doesn't trust you,' he says. 'Why do you think that is?'

"'Eddie doesn't trust anybody?'

"*Petrov laughs but shoves me away. He nods to Shrager. This time I take the hit across the jaw. The blow puts me flat on my ass. That makes Gilmore laugh.*

"'*Enough, Eddie,*' *Petrov says. Eddie steps back.*

"'*This is uncalled for,*' *I say, keeping my eyes on Petrov, swallowing blood from the punch rather than spitting it out—an act Petrov would probably take as disrespectful. 'I've got nothing to hide, and I'm betting Gilmore knows it. He's just doesn't like me.*'

"*Gilmore says, 'I like you just fine, but I don't trust you. You never let loose. You never get drunk. You never talk about yourself. I don't like people with secrets. And I have a feeling you've got plenty of them.*'

"'*Why are you wasting your time here?*' *I say, looking at Petrov.*

"*Petrov reaches into his pocket, takes out what looks like a Colt Mustang XSP.*

"'*When a man I trust doesn't trust another man,*' *Petrov says, 'I need the other man to prove to me he's loyal.*'

"*I say, 'What kind of test are we talking about?*'

"'*The only kind that matters,*' *Petrov says and holds out the Colt by its barrel. 'Take it,*' *he tells me. At the same time, Eddie points a gun at my head.*

"*I don't hesitate. I grab the pistol from Petrov, release the mag into my free hand, check its capacity—a full six shots—then shove the box back into the compartment.*

"'*Now what?*' *I say.*

"*Petrov tilts his head toward Shrager. 'Shoot him.*'

"*Shrager goes rigid. 'What the fuck, boss?*'

"'*Kill him,*' *Petrov says and takes out his phone. He starts to record the actions with its camera.*

"'*This is some fucked-up shit,*' *Shrager says, stepping back, his hands up beside his head.*

"'You've got five seconds,' Petrov says to me. "Otherwise, Eddie puts one in your brain, and we all go home.'

"Shrager looks like he's about to piss his pants. 'Why are you doing this, Yuri?' he says. 'I've pissed blood for you. Worse.'

"Petrov ignores him and starts counting. 'Five ... four ... three ...'

"I turn the gun on Shrager and pull the trigger before Petrov can get to 'two.' The bullet hits the guy in the chest, dead center. I can sense more than see Gilmore flinch. Shrager takes two steps back, looking down at his blood-soaked shirt, clawing at the buttons as if ripping them open would pull the bullet out and save his life. Petrov never takes his eyes off me as he reaches over for his gun and removes it from my hand. If he hadn't been wearing thick gloves, the barrel would have burned his fingers and palm. He slips the pistol into his jacket pocket and looks over at Gilmore.

'Chop him up,' he tells Eddie, referring to Shrager. 'Bury him.' Then he turns back to me, holding up his phone like a trophy. 'Now, I know you'll never fuck me.'

he buzzing of my cell on the tabletop pulled me out of Parker's story. It was Charley, calling.

"Hey," I said.

"Hey, yourself. Where are you?"

"In a bar."

"The joys of unemployment."

"I'm drinking iced tea and reading about my dad's narcotics squad." I told her about discovering the journals.

"Anything interesting?"

"All of it's interesting. A window into his thought process I never got from talking to him."

"You think the journals are what the killer might have been looking for?"

"Could be," I said. "Hard to tell yet. I've barely started. There are twenty in all. That's a lot of entries." I set the journal down. "How are you?"

"Good," she said. "I may have a new job. Investigative work for a law firm in Westwood. Bullock, Crane, and Treadwell."

"Never heard of them."

"Nobody has yet. They're brand new. Three 30-something women who decided to ditch their firms to form their own practice. They specialize in defending celebrities."

"And you'd be doing the dirty work. Like in that TV show, Ray Donovan."

"More like the woman who finds the people for Ray Donovan to handle."

"Lena."

"Yeah, her. I'll be like Lena. Only in real life."

"How'd you find out about the gig?"

"They called. One of their clients recommended me."

"Who?"

"They wouldn't say."

"You're not at all curious?"

"Of course, I am, but confidentiality, remember?"

"Are you happy about it?" I asked.

"The pay's good. And I'd actually be investigating stuff, not spending most of my time and energy worrying about protecting hotel guests, like I had to do at the Sunset Club."

"If you want to go back to investigating, I've got a better idea." I often urged her to return to the sheriff's department.

"Don't start," she said.

"We could be a team again."

"You're not even back. You told me this was just consulting. A favor to Ellison."

"Knowing you'd be my partner would change that."

"I already am your partner, where it counts. Besides, working together is what got us into trouble in the first place, remember? I don't want to blow things this go-round."

"Maybe it would be better now. We've learned from our mistakes."

"Stop. I'm not having this conversation with you. But I

will come have a drink. Where are you exactly? I hate the thought of you boozing alone."

"I told you; it's only iced tea," I said, looking at my watch. "And I'm running late. Unger and I have a scheduled interview with Armando Trujillo in twenty minutes. I got so caught up in reading, I lost track of time."

"You're already interviewing people? See, you *are* back."

"I'm just trying to find out how involved my dad was in all this. I'm hoping it's only peripherally, in which case, I'll let Unger run with things. Then I'll have time to drink in the afternoons."

"You're such a lush. Hurry on, then. Go do your interview that isn't about doing the job."

"You're jealous. You want to come back; you know it."

"Bye, Jagger. Good luck." Charley ended the call.

I packed up the journals and took an Uber home, so I could stash the journals and get my car. I called Unger on the way, to tell him I was running late but would be there soon.

ARMANDO TRUJILLO HID OUT IN A ONE-BEDROOM APARTMENT in Van Nuys, not far from the courthouse. It was a shithole, with a grimy, beige carpet, water-stained walls, and a smell of mildew that seemed years old. The unlucky deputy assigned to keep an eye on him let me in with a barely audible, "How ya doin'?", then went back to his chair and car magazine.

Trujillo sat on the sofa, watching a ball game on a widescreen TV. There was caution in his body language and paranoia in his eyes. He had the gaunt appearance seven years in prison can give a man. He wore jeans and a Dodgers

T and had a wooden crucifix on a leather strap hanging around his neck. He caught me staring at it.

"I found Jesus inside," he said. "Or rather, Jesus found me." He touched the crucifix then subtly made the sign of the cross with his fingers. "I haven't been able to sleep since I heard about Bags and Trane."

"Bags and Trane?" I said. "What does that mean?"

"Nicknames. We all had them, everyone in the crew, so that we never had to use real names when communicating if we thought we were being monitored. Jazz musicians. It was Parker's idea. He loved jazz the way you love rock-and-roll. I was Bird. Paula, Lady Day. Alex was Bags."

"And Parker was Trane?" I said.

Trujillo nodded and again made the sign of the cross. "*Que descansen en paz.*" *May they rest in peace.*

"What about my dad? Did he have one?"

Trujillo shook his head. "This was *our* code. When we were working the stuff on the wrong side, know what I mean?" It clearly pained him to talk about it.

I had met Trujillo a few times over the years when Dad had the crew over to the house for a card game or a barbecue. He was the oldest member on the team after my father and always seemed the most civilized.

"That poor family," he said. "*Dios Mio.* In your old home, no less. What a tragedy. What horror."

"Yes, it was," I said.

"Just Paula and me now," he said and drank from a can of Coke. "Why do you think somebody's killing us off?"

"Why do *you* think it?" I countered.

"Revenge, maybe. Petrov, coming after us for destroying his empire." He shrugged. "Paula thinks it's about money."

"Petrov's money? What's your theory on that?" I asked.

"I don't have one," Trujillo said. "There was no cash or

drugs when we did the sweep and busted Petrov. Maybe it was all bullshit and never existed."

"Parker claimed it did," I said.

"Trane said a lot of things to make himself look good. He was the worst of us when it came to bending the law. He didn't give a shit about anything. He'd steal from everybody. Shot a guy to protect his cover. You even worked the case. Ian Shrager. Remember him?"

I nodded. "Did Parker or any of you suspect Eddie Gilmore was really an undercover task force agent?"

"We didn't, and if Parker did, he never said anything."

"Any chance Gilmore knew about Petrov's stash?" Unger asked.

"Sure," Trujillo said. "He was undercover, same as Trane. And he was behind Trane shooting Shrager. Probably to have something on him. Trane could've seen it. Who knows? Maybe Gilmore's the one doing the killing, thinking one of us hid the shit away before we went to jail. Do me a favor: stop him before he gets to me. I don't want to die for something I don't even know about."

"One last question," I said. "If you hadn't gotten caught, would you have kept going?"

"Nah, I don't think so. I was tired. I wanted to get out. We all did. We talked about it. When you're dirty, you're always only one step ahead of getting caught, and it wears you out. I wanted to go back to El Salvador. Paula wanted to move to Barcelona if she left. Alex was just happy being married. I envied him. He loved Sylvia so much. *It was all for her*, he'd say, to give her the best life he could. And look what happened. Your intentions never matter." Trujillo slumped back against the sofa. "I was sorry to hear about what happened to your father. I know it's kind of late to give you condolences."

"Thank you," I said. "They're appreciated."

"We let Scotty down. He wasn't part of any of it. You know that, right? I mean, sure, he took the occasional bribe. Nobody would've trusted him otherwise. And sometimes he had to play along with the bigger stuff. But mostly, it was us in the field and him working behind the scenes. A good cop, Scotty was. A good man. Honorable. I want you to know that. I want to tell you that to your face, so there's no confusion."

It sounded rehearsed to me, like Trujillo had prepared this speech once he knew we were coming to talk to him. It was reminiscent of the things they all said during the hearing. Sometimes, people repeat things because they're true. Sometimes, they do it because it's a lie they need to maintain. As much as I wanted to, I couldn't take his words at face value.

"We were all good cops in our way," Trujillo said, "no matter what people think."

Unger scoffed. "How do you figure that?"

"We put a lot of bad people away," Trujillo said. "Sure, the lines got blurred, but it's not like we were the first ones to ever do bad things in our line of work. The end justifies the means, we always said."

"Even if the means turned you into scumbags?" Unger said.

"We've got a saying in Spanish. *Ladron que roba ladron tiene cien años de perdon.*"

"What the fuck does that mean?" Unger said.

"A thief who steals from a thief has a hundred-year pardon," I said, translating. I'd heard the phrase many times over the years but never felt there was much truth to it. With the comment, Trujillo wanted to justify his sins. And maybe the sins of my old man, as well.

17

Trane parked his car in front of a drive-thru Starbucks and walked around the corner to the Woodland Hills apartment building where Ziggy Marks and Heather Oda lived and worked. He had used the duo for years, even before he joined Scotty's operation. They were as good with computers and tracking info as anyone he'd ever known.

Their living room looked like a hacker's paradise. Six monitors connected to various laptops and servers were lined up along a worktable that stretched along an entire wall, with red, yellow, green, blue, and black cables covering the floor beneath it. Data danced across the screens. Heather sat cross-legged on a beanbag chair near an open patio sliding door, her fingers moving furiously across the keys of a MacBook Air adorned with stickers of manga characters and crudely drawn phallic symbols. A pair of red Beats headphones covered her ears, and her eyes were glued to one of the larger monitors. Her purple and green hair was buzzed on one side and hung long on the other, with bangs down in her face and piercings on her ears, nose, and an eyebrow. A large marijuana blunt smoldered in a turtle shell ashtray on the floor beside her.

Ziggy was in the adjacent kitchen, cooking something in a wok that smelled of curry. Music played from the crap speaker of his phone on the counter; it sounded like the soundtrack of *A Clockwork Orange*. He wore a bright-blue windbreaker over a *Lost Highway* T-shirt and white shorts. A thin sheen of sweat covered his bald head.

"What's up, Jazzman?" he said, running a hand across his pate. "Welcome back."

Heather glanced over and waved, then turned back to the monitor and her keyboard.

"I need you to get me some info," Trane said and placed a stuffed manila envelope folded into thirds on the counter between the kitchen and the small dining room area. "All the information's in here and your usual fee. Three K."

"Cool," Ziggy said. "Want some curry tofu?"

"I can't stay."

Heather took off her headphones. "You tell him the problem?" she asked Ziggy.

"What problem?" Trane said.

"There's no problem," Ziggy said, shaking his head and rolling his eyes. "She's such a drama queen."

Trane looked at Heather. "What's wrong?"

"Scotty's old boss called," she said. "Captain Telluride."

"Teller," Ziggy corrected. "And he's an ex-captain. Retired, remember?"

"What did he want?" Trane asked.

"To know if we'd been contacted by any of Scotty's old team. Said you guys were out of prison, and there was some shit going on about dead families and partners. I was pretty high, so a lot of it didn't make any sense."

"What did you tell him?"

"Nothing," Ziggy said. "She told him nothing. He's no friend of ours. Never was. I said we were out of that game, that we'd found God, and given up on cyber."

Heather laughed. "That's us. God loving and cyber free. Let's make T-shirts."

Her high-pitched cackling grated on Trane's nerves. "That's all he wanted to know?" he asked.

"He told me to call him if I heard from any of you." Ziggy picked up the envelope and put it into a kitchen drawer. "Which I won't because I haven't, right?"

"Good." Still, it troubled Trane that Teller was snooping around.

"How do we get in touch with you?" Heather asked.

"It's all in the packet," Trane said.

Ziggy nodded. He grabbed a fork, speared a piece of tofu from the wok, and popped the food in his mouth. As he munched, he smiled and asked, "You sure you don't want any of this?"

TRANE CRUISED SLOWLY PAST TELLER'S HOUSE. IT WAS SET back from the road, with a large, open grass yard in front. Walls divided the land from neighboring properties on each side. Trane found this problematic: he had no way of approaching without being seen, and there was no way to tell where Teller was inside the house. He assumed the old man was home; a newer-model pickup truck sat parked under a portico. Trane could wait for Teller to leave and then break in, but the ex-captain was an elderly retiree, so maybe he hardly ever left.

The whole situation annoyed and frustrated Trane. What was Teller after? How much could he know? Scotty and he were friends and would often hang out, drinking. *En vino veritas.* Scotty possibly confided things in him. Things like where he might have hidden a large amount of cash. Or what he might have done to protect a certain female.

Maybe this was a blessing in disguise.

If Trane could just come up with a way to lure the guy out.

18

Ellison's team had Paula Ramirez concealed in a motel on Fairfax, in West Hollywood, in a room at the end of a second-floor exterior corridor lined with doors. Even more depressing than Trujillo's hideout, this one had furnishings that looked unchanged since the late 1970s: green-and-brown striped upholstery on the sofa and matching chair, grimy with food stains and fingerprints; a round dinette table and chairs of chipped Formica and torn brown Naugahyde; years of dust and cigarette smoke saturating the walls and carpet.

The cop assigned to Paula, a deputy named Monroe, sat in a corner, drinking coffee and watching a ballgame on his phone, while Unger and I spoke with Paula. The sound of traffic was loud through the open window.

Prison wasn't as unkind to the only woman on my dad's team as it was to Trujillo. She looked strong and vibrant, with color in her cheeks and alertness in her eyes. She appeared rested and calm, not at all afraid that she might be the next target of a killer.

"Alex and Parker were killed because they got careless,"

she said, lighting a cigarette and blowing smoke out the side of her mouth. Her brown hair hung down in loose curls around her angular face and cascaded over her shoulders. She was thin but muscular. The only signs of seven years of incarceration were the green tattoos covering her forearms. "They let the killer into their homes, for Christ's sake."

"That merely indicates they knew the perp," I said. "And trusted him."

"People trust the wrong things all the time."

"Who do you think is responsible?" Unger asked.

Paula sucked on her cigarette, took it from her lips, and flicked ashes onto the maroon carpet. "Could be any number of people. We made a lot of enemies over the years. What's Bird saying?"

"Trujillo? He doesn't know," I said. "Maybe Petrov, out for revenge."

"Petrov would never be so obvious. He'd just make us disappear, quietly, without evidence."

"Talk to us about Eddie Gilmore."

"That asshole? He fucked us over. Goddamned task force. He worked Parker, and Parker thought it was the other way around. It never made sense to me either. Parker was smarter than that."

"Any chance Gilmore and Parker were in collusion?"

"Over what?"

"Five million dollars."

"Oh yeah, Petrov's missing money. That was bullshit. All in Parker's mind. When we went in to nab Petrov, there was no money to take."

"We're thinking it might have been removed before the bust," Unger said.

"Parker got screwed over like the rest of us."

"Is that how you see it?" I asked. "That you go screwed over? You're a victim?"

Paula frowned sarcastically. "Don't judge me, Jason. Arrogance is the only way I can get up in the morning."

"We were talking about Eddie Gilmore," Unger said.

"Forget him. He was a punk. He maybe could've taken on that family and Alex if he caught him unprepared or used his wife as leverage. But he'd be no match for Parker." Paula stubbed the half-smoked cigarette out on the sole of her shoe, then put the butt back into a packet on the table. "God, what a mess. I should've left town the minute I got out of prison."

"Where would you have gone?" I asked.

Paula smiled. "Barcelona." Then she sighed. "That was the idea back when I had money to dream big."

"How about now?" Unger said.

"I've got a brother in La Jolla. Ex-cop too. He runs a security firm. He always told me I'd have a job with him if I ever left the force."

"Even with a record?"

"Family is family."

"How dirty was my father?" I said.

She hesitated before answering. "What does it matter now?"

"I'd like to know. I've heard from some he was a saint and from others he was the devil. Chris Teller told me he was somewhere in the middle."

"That sounds about right," she said. "Nobody in vice is ever just one way. Sometimes, we get to be saints. Sometimes, we have to be devils. Most times, we're walking the line between the two. It always starts out small. You make a bust. You spot some cash in a hole in the wall or under a floorboard. You think about it, but the first couple of times, you don't take anything. Then, one day, you grab the top packet, and you shove it down your pants and walk out without saying a word. And nobody notices. And it's never mentioned. And you realize how easy it was. Plus, since you're stealing from scumbags who would kill you if they had the chance, you figure, what the hell, right?"

"I don't know," I said. "I've never faced that situation."

"Homicide's a different world."

"That's true. My dad called it after-the-fact policing."

"He's right. The damage is done. You're cleaning up and trying to put the world back in order. That's a good thing, a necessary thing. But it's not the same for us. Undercover cops live in constant hell. There is no order. Only survival."

"If you could pick one culprit behind these killings, over anyone else," I said, "who would it be?"

"Parker," she said, without hesitation. "But since he's dead, I'm guessing that's not an option."

Before I could comment, my phone buzzed with an incoming text from Captain Ellison: *Trujillo's dead, ditto police. Massacre at safe house. Watch out. Where are you?*

I looked over at Deputy Monroe. He was engrossed in his ballgame. Paula leaned forward, reaching for her pack of cigarettes on the table. I turned to Unger, who was looking at me, his brow furrowed—curious, I guess, about the text. Out of the corner of my eye, I saw a shadow pass across the blinds of the front window.

I shouted, "Get down," as a barrage of bullets pierced the top of the front door and shattered the window. I dove forward, grabbing Paula and throwing her to the floor, covering her body with my own. Unger went down on one knee, his gun out, and returned fire. Deputy Monroe did the same. A second blast from outside exploded through what was left of the window, and bullets ripped through the deputy's chest, neck, and face. The force of the shots threw him back against the wall, his vest useless to protect him from the slugs' points of entry.

Paula and I scrambled around to the other side of the sofa, putting it between us and the attack. Unger reached forward, trying to flip the coffee table up as a shield, and a bullet from the attacker's gun tore through his upper chest. The impact threw him back toward us, close enough for blood from the wound to splatter across my face.

The barrage stopped. For a moment, the room was silent, then I heard the crunch of broken glass and chipped wood—the assailant stepping inside. A magazine ejected from his gun as he reloaded. This gave me at most five seconds. I stretched out my arm and snatched Unger's pistol from the hand still clutching it. The grip was wet with his blood, the barrel warm. I popped up from behind the sofa, taking a shooter's stance, and fired three shots rapidly toward the door.

The intruder, a short, stocky man with a black ski mask over his face, caught the bullets in the forehead, neck, and shoulder. He dropped to his knees, then keeled over on his side. I stepped out from behind the sofa and approached him, my gun pointed at his head. He showed no signs of movement when I kicked his mid-section. I leaned forward cautiously and touched his neck. No pulse. He was gone.

I straightened up, turning to survey the damage. Unger lay face up a few feet from the overturned sofa, his shirt soaked with blood, his eyes wide open and vacant. The deputy sat against the wall, with his legs splayed and his head lolling forward. Blood dripped from his mouth down onto his chest. Paula was nowhere in sight.

"You okay?" I called to her.

She didn't respond, but as I slid Unger's weapon into my

waistband, I heard soft footsteps on the carpet behind me. I turned as she came at me, swinging the ceramic base of a table lamp. The glass shattered against my head. I fell back, tripping over the shooter's body, and went down. Out for the count.

WHEN I REGAINED CONSCIOUSNESS, THE SHERIFF'S department first responders had arrived, and Paula Ramirez was long gone. I told the deputies what had happened, then repeated the story for a pair of homicide detectives named Beverly and Smith. I went over it all a third time for Captain Ellison when he showed up.

The shooter carried no identification, and there was nothing in his car to tell us who he was or who had sent him. We could only hope his prints were in the system. The coroner's team came in and took away the bodies. Forensics bagged casings and the shooter's weapon. The first responding officers were dispatched to another detail forty-five minutes later, and Beverly and Smith left soon after that, along with the crime scene unit. It had been a quick sweep because the killer was present and dead, and the location was considered a department safe zone.

Ellison and I stood in the parking lot between our two cars, the last to leave.

"I'm sorry about Unger," I said. "He seemed okay, with the makings of a good detective."

Ellison nodded. "Where do you think Paula Ramirez will go?" he asked.

"La Jolla maybe." I told him about the brother. Looking up at the second floor of the motel, at the broken window and open room door, I said, "Something's bothering me."

"Only one thing?"

"Why kill Armando Trujillo and Paula Ramirez without interrogating them? Alex and Sylvia Davis, the Horton family, Colin Parker—all were tied up and probably tortured before they were killed. All three houses were torn apart during an extensive search. But these two? They were earmarked by a lone assassin who brazenly attacked a safe house guarded by cops. It doesn't match."

"Seems more like cleaning up a mess than looking for information," Ellison said. "A totally different MO."

"So maybe we're dealing with more than one enemy," I said.

"Wouldn't that suck?" He sighed. "What a mess."

"There are inconsistencies about Parker and his murder that bother me too," I said. "You get his autopsy report yet?"

Ellison shook his head. "What are you thinking?"

"I don't know, but something's off."

19

Trane parked so he had a clear view of Teller's driveway and could see the ex-captain if he left the house. With binoculars, he was able to look through a crack in the curtains of a front window and see a television on. He would sit here and wait a bit, hoping Teller had errands to run soon or maybe even a lunch with an old friend scheduled. Trane knew he couldn't just walk up to the door. As a "dead man," he didn't want to risk Teller spotting his approach from inside and taking preemptive action. The man might be old, and he might be retired, but it was a good bet his cop's instincts were still strong.

Trane decided he would wait forty-three minutes—enough time to play through Dexter Gordon's complete *Tangerine* album—and if an opportunity didn't present itself, he'd leave and rethink his plan. He felt the pressure of the timetable he faced. Soon enough, Chance and Ellison would figure out who actually died in the Sunset Strip house. Once they matched that body's DNA to Eddie Gilmore, Trane's cover would be blown. They'd have an identity to work with and a name and face to look for.

"Tangerine" gave way to "August Blues." *The temperature outside sure feels like August*, he thought, *even though it is only April*. Trane didn't mind. He liked the heat. Sweat was carnal, its stench primal. There was nothing better than sex in hot weather. God, he missed that.

Soon.

He scanned the front of the house through the binoculars. No change. No sign of movement inside. Maybe Teller wasn't home? Maybe he'd gone for a walk and forgotten to turn off the TV. Maybe that potential lunch friend had come by and picked him up. Or the guy might be dead from a stroke or heart attack, lying motionless in his bathtub or on his bed or the kitchen floor.

No way to know for sure. That frustrated the hell out of Trane.

As "The Days of Wine and Roses" ended and "The Group" began, fortune smiled: Chris Teller came out his front door and hobbled across his lawn, toward the street. The man ambled, with the help of a walking stick, and he looked in pain. But he seemed determined as he headed west, away from Trane's car, walking on the shoulder of a street without a sidewalk. At the next intersection, Teller went right, disappearing around the corner. Trane got out of the car and sprinted across Teller's front lawn to the far side of the house. He moved along the side wall. The back door had an easy lock to pick. No alarm—unless silent—sounded. Trane entered the house. He closed and re-locked the door.

Inside, he did a quick look through the home. Nothing seemed out of place. Teller was neat to the point of fastidiousness. Trane could hear the rumble of a clothes dryer and smell citrus cleaner. The pendulum of a grandfather clock in the hallway ticked away the seconds. In the study, Teller had left his older model Dell desktop computer turned on, and it hadn't gone to a screensaver yet. Trane sat and looked through the captain's recent online actions. Several browser windows were open, each to different articles from different newspapers, all local and crime related. Trane typed *Scotty Chance* into a local files search window, hoping to find something on the hard drive, but no related files came up. He scrolled through Teller's saved documents. The results were equally disappointing.

A sound from somewhere in the house, like a door clicking shut, alerted Trane. He stood, removing his gun from the holster under his arm, and headed toward the noise. He used only the balls of his feet as he stepped, staying close to the wall, minimizing the risk of creaking boards.

The back door of the kitchen was closed and locked as he had left it. The dryer in the adjacent laundry room had stopped, though he had heard no alert beep. Just outside a small window over the sink, a bird perched on the sill and stared in at him, its head cocked in curiosity. Trane looked around, listening more than watching, taking in every click, creak, shudder, and groan of the house.

He had the sense he was not alone.

Another inhabitant? Trane knew Teller was divorced and had no children. Had he taken in a woman friend? A new lover who maybe was just now getting out of bed? That would definitely change the dynamic and alter Trane's plan. Should he leave? Or go up and kill the person now before Teller returned?

Am I being paranoid? Had he only heard the dryer stop, or a draft push shut an interior door, or a branch tap against a window outside?

"Why?"

"Money, we think, stolen money. And there may be a revenge angle."

"Did Pops break the law too?" I could see by the look in my daughter's eyes how much the idea disturbed her.

"I don't know for sure," I said.

"That sucks. What a way to get pulled back."

"It is what it is. I'll deal with what I have to deal with." I stepped over to the coffeemaker. "This isn't by any chance fresh, is it?"

Charley said, "A couple of hours. You really think you need more? Didn't you just say—"

"I'm wired and exhausted all at once," I said and poured myself half a cup, then filled the mug with milk the rest of the way. "I'm going to get back to those journals. You two okay?"

"What journals?" Kathy asked.

"I found a collection of notebooks Pops kept, like a working diary. I'm hoping they contain some clues as to what's really going on now."

"We're good," Charley said. "Go back to work. Let me know if you need anything or ... just want to talk." She'd picked up that there was more to this than I'd said. She also knew not to push it in front of Kathy.

I kissed Kathy on the cheek and Charley on the lips, then went into the study with my mug of coffee. I debated doing a quick mediation session before diving in. A taste of the barely drinkable coffee made me think that was probably a good idea; I'd get more out of some transcendental meditation than drinking the bitter sludge.

I had barely settled in, ready to start, when Charley knocked and opened the door. "There's a car parked in front of the house," she said. "Not a cruiser. Civilian. Just idling. The guy behind the wheel doesn't look too friendly."

I stepped out onto the porch, my gun tucked into my back waistband. The air had cooled with the darkness. I could smell a hint of impending rain. The black Suburban that caught Charley's eye sat idling at the curb, its darkly tinted windows nearly impossible to see through. The rear passenger window glided down as I approached, revealing a man in his early fifties, with wavy blonde hair and a few days' beard growth on his chin. He wore a tan blazer over a light blue shirt, open at the collar. I recognized him right away: Jensen Vanderbrook.

"What can I do for you, Mr. Vanderbrook?" I said. "This late in the evening, outside my home."

"I apologize for the indiscretion. I was wondering if we could talk. In private." His voice was calm and smooth, his diction precise. This was a man used to making speeches and charming people.

"If it's about your son, Derek," I said, "I can't help you."

"Fifteen minutes. That's all I ask."

I glanced back at the house. Charley and Kathy stood in the study window, looking out through the Venetian blinds. I wasn't about to invite Vanderbrook into my home, but I knew if I sent him away now, I'd hear from him later. And I was curious to know what he knew or what he thought he knew.

"There's a bar around the corner," I said. "On Magnolia. A block east. Give me ten minutes."

"Thank you." Vanderbrook pressed a button and the dark window glided closed.

We can't choose the bad things that get thrown at us, I thought, heading back up to the house. *We can only bob and weave and hope we walk away unscathed.*

"Trouble?" Charley said, once I'd come in.

"Maybe not. We'll see."

"Who is that guy, Dad?"

"Nobody you should worry about. Just a holdover from the past. I'll take care of it."

THE STARLITE BAR WAS AS DARK AND MOODY AS ANY IN A 1940s film and of the same era, with wood-panel walls, a bronze-topped bar, and dark-green, round-backed stools and chairs. The clientele ranged from millennials looking for a taste of nostalgia to hardened drinkers who probably started boozing when the bar was only a decade old. Thelonious Monk played on the sound system, almost too soft to hear. It reminded me of my father. He loved Monk's music.

Jensen Vanderbrook sat alone in a corner, a glass of neat scotch or bourbon before him on the table. His driver and apparent bodyguard, a bruiser in a black suit and dark-gray turtleneck that strained against the muscles of his chest and arms, hovered near a corridor that led to the washrooms.

"Thank you for agreeing to this, Mr. Chance," Vanderbrook said. He didn't offer his hand. I'm not sure I would have taken it if he had. "And I apologize for my rather dramatic appearance at your home. I had no other way of getting your attention."

"You could get my address but not my phone number?" I said.

"I doubt you would have responded to a call."

"So you thought it better to force my hand."

"It sounds ugly when you put it that way."

"How else would you like me to put it?"

"I'm a man concerned about his child. I'd think you would have some paternal compassion."

"What is it you believe I can do for you, Mr. Vanderbrook?"

He pursed his lips as he regarded me. "Will you have a drink?" I shook my head. He frowned then lifted his glass and took a sip. "At least sit down."

I eased into the chair across from him. "Please get to the point," I said.

"When was the last time you saw my son?"

"I've never seen him." The lie flowed effortlessly. "The only dealings I had were with his partner, JoJo Sellars."

"The man you shot and killed."

"The man who took my daughter hostage and raped her."

A saw a flicker of genuine disgust in his eyes. "That was a horrible thing. Despicable. How is she doing now?"

"That's not your concern."

He nodded. Across the room, a young couple laughed at something one or the other had said. The song on the sound system changed to a vocal piece by Tony Bennett, "All in Fun."

Vanderbrook said, "I refuse to believe Derek was in any kind of partnership with a man like Joseph Sellars."

"It's your prerogative to believe or refute anything you want."

"What proof do you have he was involved?"

"It's not relevant. The case is closed. To my knowledge, the district attorney is not pursuing an investigation. They let it die along with JoJo Sellars, so wherever your son is, he's no longer the target of any official criminal pursuit. He's not on anyone's radar, if that's what concerns you."

"What concerns me is that I don't know where he is." His voice cracked with emotion as he added, "My son is missing, Mr. Chance. And you know how terrifying that feels."

"My daughter was seventeen when JoJo abducted her. From what I know, your son is twenty-four. And a deviant. A criminal."

I watched his jaw go rigid. The sadness and concern disappeared, replaced by cold anger. "You're full of shit, Mr. Chance."

"I beg your pardon?"

"You're lying as surely as you're sitting across from me. I believe you know exactly where he is."

"Do you have any evidence to substantiate that accusation?"

"Not yet." Vanderbrook stared at me with the eyes of a man who knew a thing or two about ruthlessness. He was probably superb at cards. And torture. "But I suspect you killed him. Just as you murdered Joseph Sellars."

"I shot JoJo Sellars in self-defense. And like I said, I have never met your son. I hope I never will." I stood up. "This conversation is over, Mr. Vanderbrook. Goodbye."

I turned to go, coming face to face with the bodyguard in the black suit and gray turtleneck. He was at least six-foot-five, with short black hair, and three rings piercing his left ear. "The conversation is over when Mr. Vanderbrook decides it's over," he said, putting a hand on my shoulder.

"Remove your hand," I said, holding his stare. "Do it now."

"It's all right, Andre," Vanderbrook said.

Andre took his hand away and stepped aside like a reprimanded watchdog. I turned back to Vanderbrook, softening my tone in an attempt to end this unwinnable battle of wits. "I understand your need to find out what happened to your son. Honestly, I do," I said. "But the more you dig into this, the more likely it is his illegal activities will come to light. I'll leave you to think about the ramifications of that." I walked past Andre and left the bar, hoping my words and warning had not fallen on deaf ears.

The encounter left me shaken. Sweat beaded on my forehead and ran down the back of my neck, giving me a chill. I breathed steadily to slow my heartrate. I had the unsettling feeling I hadn't heard the last from Jensen Vanderbrook, and I feared my actions regarding the disappearance of his son would not stay quiet and forgotten much longer.

21

Teller forced Trane into a chair in the study, then sat across from him with the gun pointed at his heart. Trane refused to let himself feel anger at bumbling into this predicament. He needed to keep a level head, so he could figure a way out of his unfortunate situation. The ex-captain was old and slow moving. His need for a walking cane implied arthritic problems. Trane knew he could take him down but only if he had the opportunity.

"Whose body did they find?" Teller said.

"I'll let you guess."

"Tell you the truth, I don't care, really." Teller took out his cell phone. "You're fucked, no matter what."

"Before you make that call, can I tell you something?"

"No."

"You'll want to hear this," Trane said.

"Will I?" Teller tapped in a phone number.

"I didn't come alone."

Teller chuckled. "Of course not. The fucking cavalry is waiting outside, and if you don't come out the door in the next ten minutes, they'll launch grenades and tomahawk missiles. That about right?"

"Nothing so dramatic," Trane said. "Just two well-trained men. They might have a bead on you now."

Teller hesitated. "Bullshit."

"Are you willing to take the chance?"

The phone call connected. "Sally? It's Chris Teller. Yeah, good, but I'm kind of in a crunch here. Patch me through to Jonathan Taylor, will you? It's urgent." To Trane, he said, "Empty your pockets. All of them."

Trane stood and took out his wallet, keys, cash, and a packet of chewing gum. He placed everything on a small table beside the chair. He kept glancing at the window as he did, hoping Teller would instinctively follow his gaze. All he needed was a moment of distraction.

"They won't let you get out alive," Trane said. "Even if you kill me."

"Who won't? Oh, those two guys that aren't really there. I'll take my chances. And relax: I'm not going to kill you. I'm sending you back in. This time you won't get out."

Trane nodded, frowning for effect. Again, he turned his head toward the window.

Teller said into the phone, "Yeah, I'll hold, but tell him it's urgent."

Trane looked at the window for a third time.

"What the fuck are you looking at?" Teller asked him, tilting his head toward the window.

It was a slight movement but enough. Trane lunged forward, grabbing the barrel of Teller's gun and pushing it up toward the ceiling. The gun fired, the bullet slamming into a section of crown molding. Particles of wood and plasterboard rained down. Trane kicked out at Teller's bad leg, and it buckled, the wrong way. Trane heard bone crack. Teller cried out.

Trane twisted Teller's gun hand, forcing his arm across his chest. Then Trane pushed. The gun fired a second time as Teller fell back across his desk. He knocked over the computer monitor, dropping his phone and letting go of the gun. Trane held fast to the barrel, though the heat from the shots singed the skin of his palm, and he slammed the butt down on Teller's forehead. The blow was hard enough to stun him but not render him unconscious.

Grabbing Teller's belt, Trane pulled him off the desk and threw him to the floor, face up. Trane dropped on his chest. Turning the gun around, he placed the barrel between Teller's eyes.

"Where is she?" Trane demanded. "Where's Soledad?"

"Jesus Christ! This is about her?"

Trane shifted the gun slightly and fired off a shot beside Teller's ear. The bullet tore into the carpeted floor. Teller wailed at the sound, his eyes flaring. Trane knew the closeness of the shot would most likely cause some deafness. "I asked you a question."

"She's gone! Far away, as far away as possible from you. Scotty arranged it. She told him, '*I can't be here when he gets out. I never want to see that madman again.*'"

"Liar." Trane twisted sideways and shot Teller in his good leg. The bullet shattered the kneecap. Teller screamed. "Last chance," Trane said.

"You'll never find her. Don't even try."

"I don't enjoy killing people. I'm not a monster. I'm a man who wants to find someone he loves. I know you know something. And I'll let you live. I swear to you. I don't want any more blood on my hands."

"You already have enough. You killed a little girl, you bastard."

"Just give me a name, a place, and I'll stand up and walk out of here. I'm not going to hurt her. I only want to set things right. You have my word. Don't make this your Waterloo. There's no reason for it."

Teller closed his eyes and muttered, too softly for Trane to understand his words. A prayer, perhaps. Trane got to his feet and looked around the study. From a small rolling bar, he picked up a bottle of Irish whiskey.

"Here," Trane said, kneeling down beside Teller, pulling out the bottle cork. "Have a drink." Teller eased himself up onto his elbows and let Trane put the bottle to his mouth and give him a sip. "That's better, isn't it? Now, talk to me."

"Santa Barbara," Teller said. "Scotty had a place north of there. Goleta. That's all I know."

Trane smiled. "There, see how easy that was?"

Trane took a long draw of the liquid—cheap, horrid stuff —then stood. He poured the rest of the bottle down over Teller. The man's eyes widened. He rolled onto his side, hoping to find a way to stand up. With a foot, Trane pushed Teller back down, took out a lighter, and fired it up. Then he dropped the Zippo onto the old man's chest. Teller's torso lit up like a combustion tank exploding. He screamed as the fire spread across his body. Trane stepped back but kept watching, hypnotized by the flickering, destructive dance of the orange, white, and blue flames.

"Thank you," he whispered to the burning man.

22

As I walked back home after my encounter with Vanderbrook at the bar, I tried to put myself in the man's mind frame. He was right about one thing. As a parent, I should sympathize with his desire to find out what had happened to his son. But his son was a monster. Years of work as a homicide detective had taught me this: violent men and women are rarely created in a vacuum. They grow up in an environment that propagates fury and evil. Sometimes, through nurturing: evil begetting evil, condoning it, teaching and supporting it. Other times, through oppression: the battered child becomes the battering adult. Derek Vanderbrook, I suspected, fell into the latter category. His father was an oppressor. The kind of man who would make his offspring's life hellish. And in turn, Derek became a predator.

But this was supposition on my part, and my motives for silence were selfish. I was protecting my secret. A choice I'd made to cover up a crime. Over the past two months, I had convinced myself it was the right choice, and I wasn't about to let Jensen Vanderbrook change that.

Had my father kept similar secrets? Was I now no different than him? The question festered inside me.

Back at the house, I poured three fingers' worth of bourbon into a short glass, added ice, and joined Charley on the deck. She had a goblet of white wine in her hand, half finished. We were alone in the house; Kathy had gone to visit her friend Claudia, down the street. Another sign of my daughter's journey toward healing.

"What happened?" Charley said.

"Nothing. He's looking for his son. He wanted to know if I could help. I said no. I can't afford to tell him the truth."

"You think he's going to leave it alone?"

"No." I sipped the bourbon. "But I can't worry about that. I'll deal with whatever I have to deal with when it comes along. Right now, I have other things I need to focus on." I asked if there had been any word from Captain Ellison. Charley shook her head.

"What's going on, Jagger?" she asked. "There's something else, isn't there?"

"Yeah, I didn't tell you before because I didn't want to alarm Kathy. Things went to hell during our interrogation of Paula Ramirez. Someone showed up to kill her. They took down Karl Unger and a deputy. Paula escaped."

"Was the hit part of her getaway plan?"

"I don't know. The shooter was indiscriminate. Someone went after Armando Trujillo earlier, probably the same guy. Trujillo wasn't so lucky."

"Who's the attacker?"

"We don't know yet. He's dead. I killed him. No ID. I'm hoping his prints are in the system."

"It doesn't make sense, does it?"

"No, we've got two assailants, and their motives seem at odds with each other. The first wants information. The second apparently wants to keep it from getting out. I'm betting the shooter was hired by someone else, which means they'll still be after Paula. Unless she was the one doing the hiring." I set down the glass, stood, and stretched out my arms. "Ellison wants me back on active duty immediately. Officially. No more consulting."

"With Unger dead, I'm not surprised," Charley said.

"I told him I'd only do it on one condition: you come back to work the case with me."

"Jagger! What the fuck?"

"I don't want to do this with anyone but you."

"How many times have we had this discussion? I'm not a cop anymore. I haven't been one for almost five years. Even if I wanted to, which I don't, I couldn't just say, 'Okay boys, I'm back. Where's my badge?'"

"Yes, you could, and you know it. Ellison will make it happen if you give him the go-ahead. All you have to do is say yes."

"Well, I'm saying no. I've decided to take the gig with those attorneys."

"When did you do that?"

"While you were out."

"Have you told them?"

"I was planning to call first thing in the morning."

"So don't. You can change your mind. What I'm offering is what you really want. It's what you've always wanted."

"No, it's what *you've* always wanted." She finished her wine, then set the goblet aside. "You should have talked to me before you presented this to Ellison."

"You're right, and in a perfect world, I would have. But he needed an answer, and this was what came into my head. It was my first and only condition."

"Except it's not just about you."

Charley was right, and I felt guilty over it. "At least give it some thought," I said. "Sleep on it. Promise me you'll do that."

"I can't promise you anything."

She stood and went inside. I heard the bedroom door click closed. Following her in would've made things worse. I needed to give her space. I stayed and drank bourbon, trying to figure out my next move. Then Ellison phoned and gave me one.

CALIFORNIA HIGHWAY PATROL PICKED UP PAULA RAMIREZ outside Palos Verdes on her way to her brother's house in La Jolla. They brought her back to the Valley, to an apartment in Woodland Hills on Canoga Avenue just north of Ventura Boulevard.

The living room of apartment 203 was furnished with a cream-colored couch, a grey armchair recliner, one end table supporting a knockoff Tiffany lamp, and a 32-inch flat-screen TV on a low stand by the front window. Paula stood in the open sliding glass door that led to the patio, smoking a cigarette and staring out at the night. She looked weaker, more haggard than when I'd last seen her.

"I can't get anyone to tell me if those other cops made it or not," she said, seeing me.

"You could've waited around to find out," I said.

"Yeah, well ... What can I say? Instinct kicked in. I saw an opportunity."

I asked the deputy to wait outside, telling him I needed to speak with Ramirez in private. He shrugged and nodded and stepped out the front door while punching a number into his cell phone.

"Forget making a call," I told him. "Keep alert. These people aren't messing around. They could be back."

The deputy scowled and shoved his phone into his pocket as he closed the door.

"Are you trying to scare me?" Paula said.

"Yep."

"I guess I never should've mentioned my brother and La Jolla."

"We'd have figured it out anyway," I said. "Or the killer would have. Why'd you run? You weren't a prisoner. We were keeping you there to protect you." The moment I said it, I realized how foolish it sounded. Her look confirmed this.

She sucked in smoke like a desperate addict. "How's your head?"

"I'll live."

"Sorry, I owe you for putting down the shooter. You saved my life."

"If I'd had my gun with me, maybe I could have saved Karl Unger and Deputy Monroe."

"So they are dead." I didn't respond, but Paula said, "You save what you can, Jason. Feel good that you're still alive."

I pulled two chairs from the dinette table over to the patio door, and we sat. "Tell me more about Colin Parker. Why do you think he might've been the one who took Petrov's money?"

"What difference does it make?"

"Maybe he had a plan. A partner. Or maybe it wasn't Parker who burned up in that house."

"Jesus, you think that?" Paula blew out smoke, staring at me. The idea that Parker was the one after her seemed to make her more frightened.

"I'm trying to keep you alive," I said. "Anything you say, anything you know might be helpful."

"Shit. You're not going to like what you hear."

"Doesn't matter if I do or not."

"You say that now." She paused. "There was a woman. Parker got involved with her. I think your father dropped the hammer on us, so he could make sure Parker got sent away, just to keep them apart."

"Who was she? Why would my dad care?"

"Her name is Soledad Varela, and she's Scotty's daughter."

23

I drove back home, blasting Marilyn Manson's "Heaven Upside Down," processing the revelation. Learning the news my father had a daughter out there shouldn't have shocked me. He'd been a philanderer while my mother was alive. I doubt his sexual appetite waned after she died. If anything, it probably intensified. It didn't surprise me he had kept her a secret either. Clearly, he never intended nor wanted us to meet.

I slipped in the front door of the dark, silent house, re-set the alarm, then took a can of Coke from the fridge, and went into my study. Sitting at my desk, I did an Internet search for Soledad Varela. It rewarded me with a lengthy series of links to various women around the world, some connecting me to Facebook pages, others to LinkedIn, still others to Twitter. None of the many women in the pictures looked familiar. Why should they? To my knowledge, I'd never laid eyes on Soledad Varela. I could be staring her right in the face and not know.

What most interested me was her potential connection to Colin Parker and the fact that my father might have sent

Parker to jail because of her. My suspicion that Parker was alive and behind the recent murders intensified.

JUNE 17, 2010—SC PERSONAL FILES. NOT FOR OFFICIAL EYES.

Well, I guess it had to catch up with me. Nobody can screw around as much as I have, usually without caution or care, and not worry that one day, he'll get a phone call, letter, or a knock on the door. Of course, suspecting *and* expecting *are very different things. Sure, a vague concern followed me around over the years, mostly catching up with me late on a sleepless night. I'd think about it, fret a little, then dismiss it and get on with my life.*

Until the past showed up at my door.

Her name is Soledad. I'd met her mom, Leticia, way back in 1990, while we were going after her ex-husband, Carlos Varela. I was just a detective then, working in a unit run by Chris Teller. I interviewed Leticia several times over the course of the investigation. We had three, maybe four extracurricular encounters. She was beautiful and bright and sexy as fuck. Who's going to say no? Then the case ended, and we put Carlos away for life. Leticia relocated up north. I shifted focus to other investigations. Eventually, Teller was promoted to captain, and I took charge of the undercover unit. I forgot about Leticia for twenty years. Now, one of those three or four encounters has brought her back into my life.

THIS SECTION OF MY FATHER'S JOURNAL READ LIKE MORE OF A confession than anything he'd written so far. But a confession to whom? Had these journals been written for me? If so, why hide them in a forgotten trunk in our attic? Maybe he just needed to get it all out, an admission to himself, a way of remembering his experiences with no intention of ever sharing them.

JULY 7, 2010 —SC PERSONAL FILES. NOT FOR OFFICIAL EYES.

Letty brought Soledad to meet me last night. She's a beautiful young thing, barely 19, with the same dark hair and haunting eyes as her mom. Carlos, I learned, died in prison, three months after Soledad was born. He never met her. Had no reason to, Letty said. There was no way, she claimed, he could be the father because she hadn't had sex with him for six months when she met me, and I was the only one she'd slept with when she got pregnant. She never wanted to let me know, never wanted to burden me with something I didn't expect or probably want. "So why now?" I asked her. She told me she'd secretly hidden money away over the years while preparing for the divorce. They'd survived on it these last nineteen years, but even the largest fortunes dry up if you don't keep feeding them.

So Letty needed money and came to me looking for it. She was ashamed, she said, but had no one else to turn to. "It's only for our daughter," she told me. I said I needed the proof of a paternity test done before I'd consider helping out. Letty must have expected that; she agreed without hesitation. I knew then, with or without any test, this was no scam. I was looking into the eyes of my daughter—one whom for nineteen years I'd had no idea existed.

JULY 22, 2010 —SC PERSONAL FILES. NOT FOR OFFICIAL EYES.

The test came back positive, as I knew it would. I had money saved—for Jason, for Kathy—and I took some of it out and gave it to Leticia. Two days ago, as they were packing to go back north, Letty suffered a massive stroke and died on her way to the hospital. Soledad's in shock, the poor girl. Now she's got no one. I've decided to set her up in an apartment the team sometimes uses for meetings or interrogating CIs while I figure out what to do next. I'm ashamed to admit that I'm embarrassed to tell Jason. He's on a right, smart track and is already one hell of a detective though he's only been at it a couple of years. I don't want to imagine the judgmental look in his eyes and especially in little Kathy's if they learn about Soledad. I was still married to Jason's mother, Evie, when she was conceived. I'll do my duty; I'll take care of this new daughter in my life, but it will be my private doing. My secret. A penance for being so damned unfaithful.

"YOU OKAY?"

I turned toward the voice and saw Charley in the doorway. She looked disoriented, like she'd just woken up.

"I'm fine. Are you?"

She shrugged, stepping into the room. "Stupid nightmare. We were on a stakeout, and you got shot." She sat across from me on the small sofa. "It's your fault."

"That I got shot?"

"No, that you've got me thinking about being a cop again." She looked at the black-and-white notebook in my hand. "Still at it?"

"Can't seem to help myself."

"Anything interesting?"

"Dad had a daughter. A woman named Soledad Varela."

"No shit."

"My reaction too."

"You didn't know?"

"Never once heard about her."

"Who's the mom?"

"A lady named Leticia Varela. He had an affair with her after he sent her husband to prison, and he didn't meet Soledad until she was nineteen. He kept this whole side of his life a secret."

"Where is she now?"

"I don't know. Leticia died seven years ago. Soledad would be twenty-six now. According to Paula Ramirez, she got involved with Colin Parker, and Dad didn't approve. Paula thinks he may have turned on the team just to make sure Parker went to jail."

"Turned on the team. You mean he fabricated evidence to send them away?"

"No, I don't think so. They all copped to the crimes at the time, and the evidence against the team was solid. They were guilty, no question. I think Paula means my father threw them all to the wolves to get rid of Parker. He might have even been cooperating with the task force that sent Eddie Gilmore in. I've found nothing yet to back it up, but consider this: what if he's the one killing them off?"

"Your dad?"

"No, dummy. Parker."

"Same difference. Both are dead. Where's Eddie Gilmore?"

"Disappeared."

"Then I'd be looking for him."

"I think that's exactly what we're supposed to believe. Colin Parker's body was burned to a crisp, and the MO doesn't match the later killings. That's bothered me all along. Plus, there were personality inconsistencies at the scene. Parker was a jazz nut, like my old man. Had a poster of Coltrane on his wall and a collection of jazz vinyl that, if it had survived the fire, would probably be worth tens of thousands of dollars."

"So?"

"The body they found had a skull ring and an earring of a hand with the thumb and pinky extended, the mark of the devil."

"I'm still not catching up," Charley said.

"Both are common to metal heads. Rock-and-roll."

"So he liked both."

"Maybe, but I've never known a jazz purist who could sit through a single Rammstein song. They venture into some rock but usually draw the line at heavy metal."

"You're such a bigot," she joked, but I could see the intrigue in her eyes. She was following along, *catching up*, and liked what she was hearing.

"And there's something about the physicality of the body," I said. "The guy that burned to death in Parker's house was tall and thin. I remember Parker being a broad, muscular man."

"The fire probably charred away some of his flesh."

"There's a delightful image." I paused. "I could be way off the mark. But what's a better cover than death?"

She considered this. "Let's say you're right. What's Parker's game plan?"

"Find Soledad, I'm thinking. If she's off the radar, maybe it's because my dad arranged to make her disappear. Parker's sentence was finite. If Dad was willing to send him to jail to protect her, then it meant he'd go to equally extreme lengths to keep her safe when Parker got out."

"So that's the reason your father's house was the first hit," Charley said, "Parker was looking for information about her whereabouts."

"Right, now it makes sense." I checked the time. Almost

4 a.m. The sun would be creeping up in another couple of hours.

"You look like you're running on fumes," Charley said. "You need to get some sleep."

"I doubt I could close my eyes. The one person who might could shed light on this is Evelyn, Dad's housekeeper. She'll be up by five. I'll call her then."

"That's an hour away. Come on. At least pretend to get some sleep."

She took my hand and led me to the bedroom. I didn't resist.

WE LAY IN BED IN THE DARKNESS, MY ARM AROUND HER NECK and her head resting on my chest.

"It's weird," I said. "When I was a kid and even a teen, my dad told me everything. His cases, his fears, even his shames. The women, the drinking. All of it. He never held back. And not in a bragging way. He always sounded regretful. Part confession, part warning. Like he was teaching me a lesson. How not to live my life. Once I became a cop, though, it all stopped. He closed up. All he wanted was to hear my stories."

"It was your turn," Charley said. "He was proud."

"It would sure be nice to think that way."

"You've no reason to believe otherwise."

"At a point, I started wondering if he stopped telling me things because he'd grown ashamed of something. You know, that one thing you did that maybe went too far. I decided it was better not to know. That's the reason I didn't want to take this case at first. I didn't want to learn something that might change the way I felt about him."

"Knowing something new doesn't have to change things," Charley said.

"Except it will."

"Do you want to stop?"

"I can't," I said. "I'm in too deep. And not just because of my dad. I didn't realize until I was back in the thick of it just how much I need this. I don't know how to do anything but investigate." I rolled on my side to look at her. She leaned in and kissed me, and I responded. I needed, if only for a moment or two, to get lost in her arms, her kisses, in making love, so I could stop thinking about the past and that lost space in which my life now hovered.

24

To Trane, the journey north so early in the morning felt like traveling through a ghost world. Darkness. Silence. Emptiness. Then, suddenly, an ambulance raced past, heading the other direction, its red lights flashing and siren bleating like a wounded animal, disturbing the solitude of the night. On its way to rescue someone in trouble, maybe even dying. So much death in this city of desperation.

And I'm the cause of some of it, he thought. The notion gave him no satisfaction. What a mess.

Trujillo dead, Paula missing. It seemed Trane had competition. Someone else after the same thing? Or someone trying to stop him from learning anything? More than likely, the latter. At least Ziggy and Heather had done well with their assignment; they'd found a Wells Fargo account in Scotty's and Jason's names used to pay online utility bills on a property in Goleta, north of Santa Barbara. This confirmed Teller's admission before he died. *The fucker had been honest, after all.*

Payments were being made from the account to local gas

and electric companies and a home security firm, which meant there would be an alarm. Money was also paid to someone named Evelyn Marbut. Trane guessed she was a housekeeper.

In hindsight, it seemed so obvious. Why wouldn't Scotty have at least one other property set up somewhere? A safe location if things ever got too hot. Trane owned one in El Paso, where he could walk across the border into Mexico and disappear into another life if the situation ever called for it. Paula had a condo in La Jolla, near her brother. Trujillo once said he had bought a small place somewhere in El Salvador. Only Alex chose not to invest in an escape route. He must have figured he would never need it, that he was invincible.

It never ceased to amaze Trane how wrong people can be about their destiny.

THE LAST BEAUTIFUL STRAINS OF "VISITOR FROM NOWHERE" by Herbie Hancock and Wayne Shorter played as Trane pulled into the lot of a small motel on Coastline Drive in Santa Barbara. The odor of sulfur competed with the smell of the sea as he walked past the courtyard pool. Leaves floated on the water's surface, dark masses against the pool's underwater lights. A broken gate that led to the alley behind the hotel clanged in the wind.

Trane checked in, paying cash, then took the exterior stairs to the second floor to room 201. He placed a "Do Not Disturb" card on his doorknob, slid the security bar of the door into place, closed the curtains, then sat on the bed, and connected his phone to the free motel wi-fi.

He fed Scotty's Goleta address into Google Maps, then switched to satellite view and zoomed in on the cabin. The place appeared to be a converted ranger's station, nestled away in the hills, hidden from the outside world. He input another address and learned that Evelyn Marbut's house was less than ten minutes from the motel.

SHE LIVED IN A SMALL SPANISH REVIVAL HOUSE NEAR THE mission. Its lawn was more dirt than grass. A stone path led to the porch, where floral vines long dead hung from the roof, forming a curtain of brown strands. No alarm beeped or blared when Trane picked the front door lock and entered the home.

The living room was neat but run down: old furniture, generic paintings on the walls, and a lack of personal items anywhere. To the right, an archway led to the kitchen. On the left, another led to a short corridor with a door on each side. He smelled brewing coffee and heard a shower running. It was just past four in the morning; Evelyn was an early riser. Across from the bathroom, the second door opened to the single bedroom. One side of the bed was neat, the other rumpled and unoccupied. Evelyn Marbut slept alone.

The kitchen was organized but not clean. There was dust across the floor and stains on the cabinet faces. Built-up grease surrounded the burner grates on the stovetop and the exhaust fan. Under the aroma of coffee, traces of last night's dinner lingered, something with onions and beef. The dishes in the cabinets were clean and arranged in an orderly fashion. Trane found a mug and poured himself a cup of coffee. He drank it black, grimacing at its mediocrity, but it would have to suffice.

Eventually, Evelyn came into the kitchen, her hair wet from the shower. She wore a thick, fraying terrycloth robe. If seeing him sitting at the table, with his gun laying out on its top, frightened her, she never let on.

"I don't have much cash," she said, holding his gaze with steely eyes.

"I'm not here for that," Trane said. "I need the keys and security code to Scotty Chance's cabin."

Her brow furrowed. "I don't have them anymore," she said. "Scotty's been dead for six years."

"Payments are still made to the utilities companies from his account. And to you. Don't insult my intelligence. All I want is access. Give it to me, and I'll be on my way."

After a pause, she said, "Why should I?"

Trane chuckled, impressed with her feistiness. "Scotty had something that belonged to me. It's time I took it back. What that is does not concern you. Please don't make this more complicated than it needs to be."

Evelyn never changed her stance. She held her head high, her jaw firm, and kept her hands in the pockets of the robe. She was a proud woman, even when fearful. Trane admired that.

"I don't want to hurt you," he said. "And there's no reason for this to go that way. As long as you cooperate. You can't betray a dead man, can you?"

"If I give you what you want, you're still going to kill me."

"What makes you think that?"

"I know your kind."

Trane smiled. "No, you don't." He set the coffee mug down. "I'll make you a deal. Do three things for me, and I won't even hurt you, I promise."

"What things?"

"Give me the key and access code. That's one. Promise that you'll leave today and go back to Wisconsin. That's two."

"And the third thing?"

"I'll ask you a simple question. If you answer correctly, our business here is done."

"What question?"

"Get the key first. I need to know I can trust you too."

She paused. "I have to leave the room to get it."

"Go ahead."

Evelyn stepped out to the foyer. She came back a moment later, holding a set of keys on a small silver hoop. She placed them on the table.

"Good," he said. "Thank you. Now, the security code."

"Seven-eight-zero-zero. Jason's and his daughter, Kathy's birth years."

Trane was tempted to laugh. He could've figured that out on his own. Saved himself this torturous exchange. Simply kill Evelyn Marbut while she was in the shower, take her keys, and leave. It could've been so easy.

"Do you need me to write it down for you?" she asked.

"No, it's easy enough. I'll remember. Do you promise you'll leave town?"

"Yes."

"Good. Now, the question. Tell me who played tenor sax on Miles Davis's landmark recording 'Kind of Blue.'"

She stared at him, confused. "I don't know about things like that."

"I'll give you a hint. *Love Supreme* is his most famous album as a solo artist."

"Please, I'm not that into music, especially not jazz."

"Ah, but see? You knew I was talking about jazz. I bet you know the answer too. Deep down. Close your eyes, and think about it. His name will come to you."

"No, I ... Can't you ask me something else?"

"Only a handful of sax players achieved mass recognition. Charlie Parker is the most famous, but he played alto. The answer to my question is the most famous tenor man."

Evelyn put her hands on the back of a kitchen table chair and gripped the wood. Her arms trembled. "Why are you doing this? I gave you the information you wanted, and I promised I'd leave today. Back to Wisconsin. I'll never return."

"I'm sure of that." Trane sipped coffee. "Take a guess. It'll be fun."

Her eyes roamed the space as she tried to think of the right answer. "Kenny G," she finally said. From her sad, frightened expression, Trane could tell she knew she was wrong.

"Sorry, no. I'll give you one more shot."

"I swear I don't know. I'm ignorant about those kinds of things." Evelyn teared up. Her fingers had turned white clutching the chair back. Her feistiness had dissolved into fear. "I'm an old lady. I don't know culture. I don't listen to music. I don't read books. I just ... I watch TV. You could ask me something about that, and I bet I could answer it."

"What a shame," he said. "What a waste." He stood. "You must lead a very sad life if your only entertainment comes from television." She flinched as he reached into his pocket.

Trane laughed. "Relax. I'm just getting out my phone. I keep music on it. I want to give you a treat."

He woke the cell up, then flicked through the screen until he found what he was looking for. He hit play. "So What" came out of the small speaker.

"This is the first track off the album *Kind of Blue*. The Miles Davis Sextet. That's Bill Evans on piano." Trane closed his eyes, listening to the music, loving it, even in its bad-quality playback. He never tired of this album. "It's the most successful jazz recording of all time. A perfect synergy of talent and creativity. Simple yet so complex. Can you feel it? Do you agree?"

"It's very beautiful, yes," Evelyn said.

"See all that you've been missing? Okay. Here comes Miles. There. Hear him on the trumpet? I wish I had headphones for you. It's a pity your first time has to be in such mediocre fashion."

"It's ... really nice. Thank you for sharing with me."

Her gratitude sounded sincere, and this delighted him. "Evelyn, it's my pleasure. Truly. Ah, and here he is. The answer to my question. John Coltrane. They called him Trane. That's also my nickname." He lifted the phone closer to her ear. "So perfect, so magical, don't you think?"

"It's very beautiful." She was crying now, though Trane knew the tears were not brought on by the music. At least the last thing she would hear would be something profound. Trane believed everyone should die listening to beautiful music.

25

I woke from a light slumber—more a dazed state than actual sleep—to a subtle, clicking sound coming from the other side of the house. Having lived here for five years, I knew the normal creaks and groans the building made. This was not one of them.

I sat up, glancing at the clock. The digital dial read 4:35 a.m. Dawn was still more than an hour away. Charley slept beside me, undisturbed. I stood and walked out of the bedroom, across the corridor, and into my study. A bathroom connected it with the kitchen, and there, a door led outside to the dog run. The door had two deadbolts in addition to the lock on the knob. The clicking sound came from one of them. I went back into my study and, for the second time that day, took my handgun from the desk drawer.

I disarmed the security alarm and exited the house via the front door. The cold concrete of the driveway stung my bare feet as I jogged to the fence of the dog run. Its gate stood ajar, the padlock unclasped on the ground nearby. I slinked through the cracked opening and eased my way along the garage wall, staying out of the security light to avoid casting a shadow.

At the corner, I peered around and saw a man in dark jeans and a black windbreaker hunched over the kitchen door. He had his dark baseball cap turned around, so the visor covered his neck. A small satchel rested at his feet. I jogged silently up behind him, grabbed his jacket collar, and pulled him upright, then slammed him against the door. "Drop your tools," I said. Something metallic clattered on the cement. I stepped back and leveled the gun at his back. "Lace your fingers together. Place them on the top of your head."

The intruder did as he was told, with no resistance. I kicked his satchel away, then frisked him with my free hand. He had no concealed weapons.

"Come on," I said, leading him into the backyard with a firm grip on his neck. He went without struggle or comment. I pushed him down onto a wrought iron chair and sat across the patio table from him.

"What's your name?"

He stayed mum, but his eyes darted around the perimeter of the yard.

"Forget it," I said. "There's nowhere to go. You'll save us both a lot of headache if you're straight with me. I assume you're not here to rob the place, but someone sent you to do or find something. I also assume you know who I am, so you realize you've got no option other than to cooperate. Right?"

He nodded.

"Now, what's your name?"

"Kevin."

"Last name."

"Green."

"All right, Kevin. Who sent you?"

"I don't know."

"Don't stonewall me. You're in a shitload of trouble right now."

"I mean it. I only got instructions." His voice cracked. "And money wired into my account."

"What were those instructions?"

"Break in. Search your office. Find out what you knew about somebody. I've been sitting outside that door for an hour, just waiting for you guys to go to sleep, so I could get in and out before it got light."

"Who's the somebody?" He hesitated. "You're doing fine, Kevin. Don't start fucking up. Who's the somebody?"

"I don't know. I swear. The instructions came in text messages from a phone number with no ID."

"Give me your phone."

"It won't do you any good," he said. "I erased all the texts right after I read them, and I memorized your address."

"Give me the phone anyway."

He took a smartphone out of his front pants pocket and set it on the table. I picked it up, looking at the screen. It was touch ID protected. I turned the screen toward him. "Unlock it," I said. He frowned, but put his thumb on the button. His home page came up. I opened the messages app. The folder was empty.

"Give me the phone number of whoever texted you," I said.

"I don't remember it. I swear. It was one I'd never seen before. And there were only four messages. I just paid attention to the content."

"Look and see if auto backup is set to the cloud," Kathy said. She stood barefoot on the patio, wearing loose sweat pants and a T-shirt that said, *Fuck you, you fucking fuck*. Her hair was mussed from sleep.

"Kathy, go inside," I told her.

"Dad, just check. If his phone backs up automatically, you can restore everything, including texts. As long as the backup happened after the texts came in." She stepped down from the deck and approached the table.

"I don't back anything up," Kevin said. "I wouldn't even know how to do that."

"It does it itself," Kathy said. "That's what automatic means, dipshit."

I suppressed a smile.

KATHY TALKED ME THROUGH THE BACKUP PROCESS. IT TOOK about ten minutes. While we waited, I tried to get more information from the man—about himself, his orders, and mostly the person or persons who had hired him. He had no wallet on him and no form of identification. He swore to me that he knew no more than what he'd already told me.

Once the phone finished restoring, I reopened his message app. The texts had returned, four of them, and were pretty much word for word what he'd said. No surprises. I didn't care. I wasn't after the messages. I called the originating phone number.

A youngish-sounding woman answered. "What's happened? Why are you calling me? That wasn't the arrangement."

"This is Jason Chance," I said. "Your guy was careless and got caught. Who am I speaking with?"

The woman disconnected without another word.

"Kathy, go get me the house phone, will you?" I said.

She hurried inside, past the just-exiting Charley, who was tying the cinch of her robe around her waist. She looked fresh and alert, no trace of sleep in her eyes. "A patrol car is on the way," she said.

"Good, thanks."

"Come on, man," Kevin said. "I took nothing. I was just doing a stupid job. No harm, no foul. Let me go, and you'll never see me again."

"Not gonna happen," I said.

Kathy came back out with the house phone. I made a call and had a search run on the phone number of the woman who had hired Kevin. The info came back ten minutes later: the phone was registered to Soledad Varela, with a Santa Barbara address.

PART II

A LOVE SUPREME

the porch rotted in spots, and the roof had patched-up holes that appeared makeshift and flimsy. Was that the intention to keep people away? *It must be,* Trane thought. A safe house was only safe if invisible.

He parked his Beemer at the back of the structure, out of sight from the driveway, between the cabin and a small gardening shed. The key Evelyn had given him slipped easily into the lock of the back door and turned without resistance. Trane entered a cool, dark kitchen filled with a pleasant mélange of smells: lingering soap, incense, lemon. He keyed the security code Evelyn had given him into a small pad beside the door. The soft beeping of the alarm system went silent.

The living room, rustic in style, had a brown, leather sofa with a crimson blanket thrown sloppily over its back, two mission chairs on either side of a large, wooden coffee table marred by water rings and scratches, a high-back upholstered chair under a side window, and several Navajo rugs carelessly arranged on the wood floors. The pine walls were bare, except for a large painting of a Southwestern pioneer town over the stone fireplace in the corner. Trane remembered Scotty's fascination with the Old West.

The beds in the two bedrooms were made, the floors swept. The closets were empty of anything but hangers. The bathroom was recently cleaned—presumably by Evelyn— and sparkled. There were no toiletries that would indicate anyone, especially not a woman, lived here.

Disappointed, Trane removed his jacket and slung it over a chair back, and put on a pair of latex gloves. He pulled shut the curtains throughout the cabin, blocking out the world, and then began a careful, methodical search, working his way from the front to the back of the house. He looked through every drawer and cabinet, examined every piece of paper, flipped through every book. He searched for anything that might tell him Soledad's whereabouts.

He also checked every spot where he thought Scotty might have hidden a large amount of cash: in dressers and behind bookshelves; inside the cushions of sofas, chairs, and mattresses he ripped open with his knife; in the kitchen cabinets, not caring if he broke plates and glasses. He even checked the toilet tank, thinking Scotty might have dunked some of the cash there, inside an airtight plastic bag.

There was nothing. No cash, no sign of where else it might be hidden, and most disheartening, nothing that led him to Soledad. His stomach tightened with frustrated nausea. Maybe she had relocated, as Teller warned, but did it on her own. Perhaps Scotty died not knowing where his daughter was. In that case, the odds of Trane finding her were at about zero.

What should he do? Chalk up the failure as a life lesson and move on? Could he let it all go that easily?The sound of a car door slamming outside pulled him out of his thoughts. He went over t o the front window and peeked through a crack in the curtains, careful not to ruffle the fabric as he did. His heart grew tight in his chest.

There, she stood, as intoxicating and beautiful—as perfect—as he remembered. She was dressed in white, her hair longer than it had been when he last saw her. She'd lost weight. Her eyes still glowed like fire. Soledad, his angel, his purpose, his salvation, had found him.

I called 911, identified myself, and reported Evelyn's death. The dispatcher asked if I had reason to believe there had been foul play. When I said, "Most definitely," she put me through to the local police station. I spoke with Detective Wanda Downs, who told me to wait at the house for her to arrive, so I could give a full report.

I wanted to use the time to search Evelyn's home. Technically, I had no jurisdiction to investigate a crime committed in Santa Barbara County, but I wasn't looking for evidence in Evelyn's killing. I wanted to find anything Evelyn might have that related to Soledad Varela. At the same time, I had to be careful not to disturb the scene for the local crime unit.

"I say we wait for SBPD," Charley said. "Let them do the search. Fill them in on the case. Let them find something we can use, so it doesn't bite us in the ass later."

"I'm not ready to tell them about Soledad, and clues to her whereabouts are all I'm interested in finding here."

"Okay, then. Do what you've gotta do. At your own peril."

I went to work, finding little that mattered in the living

room and kitchen and nothing related to Soledad or Colin Parker. In the bedroom closet, a suitcase I recognized as belonging to my father was stored on the shelf above Evelyn's clothes. I eased it down and set it on the floor by the bed—eerily aware of Evelyn's body nearby, irrationally fearful she might suddenly sit up and glare at me, demanding I tell her what the hell I thought I was doing.

Inside the suitcase were shirts and slacks I remembered my dad wearing and some men's clothing I'd never seen. At the bottom, along with a small travel case filled with toiletries, I found a plastic pouch containing legal documents, among them a lease copy for an apartment in Santa Barbara. The co-tenant was Soledad Varela. I committed the address to memory, closed the suitcase, and put it back on the shelf in the closet.

Two SBPD officers arrived before I could search further, with a forensics team and a slender woman with thick glasses and graying hair who identified herself as Detective Wanda Downs. She scowled the minute she entered and saw us.

"How'd you get into the house?" Down asked.

"The back door was unlocked," I said.

"Why'd you think to come in?"

"Evelyn Marbut works for me, cleaning a cabin my family's owned for many years in Goleta. I've been worried about her. She hasn't returned my calls, so my partner and I drove up to check."

Downs nodded, then asked me to lead her to the body. We went to the bedroom.

"You found her here, as she is now?" Downs said, looking at Evelyn's corpse. "You try to resuscitate her?"

"No, I checked her pulse to verify she was dead."

"You touch or move anything at all?"

"Is she in any trouble?" Dan asked.

"I can't talk about the investigation," I said. Dan frowned.

We rode the elevator to the second floor. Dan used a master key to open Soledad's apartment. It was small and cozy, with tasteful, traditional furniture throughout. A large window gave a partial view of Santa Monica Bay over the roofs of the houses across the street. Colorful prints hung on the walls, watercolor sketches of Paris and Monte Carlo. A delicate scent hung in the air, the remains of someone's perfume.

"Donna Karan," Charley said, taking a whiff. "Not cheap."

I sent Dan off, thanking him, and then told the uniformed officers we were looking for anything related to either Colin Parker or Scott Chance. "Documents, photos, addresses, information about bank accounts," I said. "The bingo card would be a recent location for Parker or any evidence of communication with him."

We divided up, the officers taking the living room and kitchen, Charley looking through the master bedroom. I focused on a second bedroom Soledad had turned into a home office. The desk drawers contained the usual: checkbook, pens, stationary, batteries of different sizes and voltages. The laptop on the desk was password protected, and I knew too little about Soledad to venture a guess.

In a leather folder in a bottom drawer, I found a collection of articles from various newspapers and magazines related to my father and the arrests of his team. Soledad had followed the case with apparent interest, collecting clippings about the trial and the indictments. She had highlighted certain sections with a yellow marker, mostly those relating to Colin Parker.

"Hey, Jagger," Charley called from the other bedroom. "Come look at this."

I joined her. She pulled out a small carry-on bag from under the bed and popped it open. Inside, clothing best suited for a trip somewhere tropical and warm was neatly packed: bathing suits, linen shorts, silk robes. A side compartment held ten thousand dollars in cash and three passports—two from the U.S. and one from Mexico—each with a different name, all three with a photo of a woman I assumed was Soledad Varela.

In the living room, a Santa Barbara officer brought in a shoe box he had found in the broom closet of the kitchen. He set it down on the coffee table. Inside, a Beretta 9mm wrapped in a red towel lay next to a half-empty box of ammo. The gun was a sheriff's department standard issue, pre-2015, the kind my father had used to kill himself. Also in the box were a plastic bag containing two police medals— one for meritorious conduct, one the sheriff's department Medal of Valor—and a sheriff's department badge with my father's name on it.

After his funeral, I had grown angry when I couldn't find these items in any of his possessions. I accused our Los Angeles housekeeper of taking them and fired her when she denied the accusation. I'd been wrong. Perhaps Dad gave Soledad the medals and the badge, but the gun had to have been stolen. How? Why?

TRANE SAT ON THE COUCH IN THE LIVING ROOM OF THE CABIN, waiting for Soledad to come in and wondering how things would play out once she did. God knows what negative ideas about him Scotty had put in her head after the arrests. Would she run to Trane, throw her arms around him, and tell him how much she had missed him? Or would fear take over and send her fleeing back out the door?

He heard no sounds from outside save the wind through the trees and the occasional seagulls' caw. No creaking on the porch as she approached. No sound of a key in the lock. Not even a car engine turning over as she changed her mind and drove off. Finally, he stood and went back to the window. The car was still there, parked in the driveway, but there was no sign of Soledad.

In the kitchen, he peeked out the window over the sink and glimpsed her walking with purpose across the side field, heading toward the rear of the property. He stepped over to the door and pulled aside its white curtain, so he could view the backyard. Soledad strode past his car, glancing at it as she removed a key ring from her jacket pocket. Then she used a key to undo a padlock on the garden shed door.

As she vanished into the darkness of the shed, Trane opened the back door and stepped outside. "Soledad," he shouted. He waited a moment and then called out, "Hello? It's me."

She reappeared in the shed doorway, looking surprised and angry. Both hands were behind her back. "What are you doing here?" she said. "How'd you find me?"

"It wasn't easy." He took a few steps toward her. "I was scared you'd left town, and I'd never find you."

"You shouldn't be here," she said. "You shouldn't have come."

Trane didn't like the fearful expression on her face or the irritated tone in her voice. "What's wrong?" he said. "I thought you'd be happy."

"Everything's changed."

"I know this has been hard for you. It's also been difficult for me. I've missed you. You have no idea how much." He took a couple more steps.

She brought her hands around in front of her, revealing a gun in one of them. She raised it up, pointing it toward him. "Stop where you are. Don't come any closer."

"Soledad? What are you doing?"

"I can't, Colin. I can't let you back in."

He saw tears in her eyes. They gave him hope. The sadness meant she still loved him. She just was scared. "Look, I get it. Scotty filled your head with bad things. But you know me, the true me. And you know what we shared. Put the gun down. Let's go inside and talk."

"There's nothing left to say."

"There's plenty. I love you, Soledad. I want to give you the life you deserve. I'm ready now. We'll take the money and go far away."

"What money? What are you talking about?"

"Yuri Petrov's money. I know Scotty took it. He never would have given it to Jason. He must have given it to you."

"I don't know what you're talking about. I don't have any money, and I can't let you back into my life."

"Don't say that. You're just confused. I understand. Please, come inside." He held a hand out to her. "There's no one else for me. Only you."

Soledad cried out as she fired two shots, aiming at his heart.

She paused and then said, "I doubt that is the reason you are here."

"I have a search warrant."

"Again, not answering my question. What do you want?"

"Colin Parker. We're looking for him, and I suspect he's looking for you."

She cocked her head to the side. "I read that Colin died in a fire."

"He didn't. He's alive. He killed a man named Eddie Gilmore and put the body in his place. He's murdered eight people since his release from prison."

"Why would you think he'd be after me?"

"Let's not play it that way, Miss Varela. You are, for the record, Soledad Varela, correct?"

She nodded, once. Outside, a cloud passed over the sun, and the room grew dark. A slant of shadow caused by the Venetian blinds sliced across her brow, obscuring her eyes. "How is it you'd like me to play it then, Mr. Chance?"

"I know about your relationship with Parker. He broke into my father's old Los Angeles home, and he killed an innocent family there. Then he tore the place apart. He was searching for something. He did the same with Alex Davis and his wife. And an ex-sheriff's captain, Chris Teller. A few hours ago, he murdered a woman who tended to my family's Goleta cabin. All the pieces connect to my father. And the one thing, other than the job, linking Parker and him is you."

Soledad stepped farther into the apartment, closing the door behind her. She set her handbag on a small table under an oval mirror. I could see her eyes in the reflection, darting around the room from one person to the next. Assessing the enemy, I imagined, gauging the threat level.

Finally, she turned to face me. "Are you placing me under arrest?"

"We don't have a reason to at this point."

"Then I could ask you all to leave."

"Yes," I said.

"But first we'd have to finish the search," one officer added.

"So do it, and please get out."

She walked toward the bedroom. I stepped in front of her, blocking her way.

"Why do you have three passports in different names?"

"That's none of your business."

"I get it. You're scared. You've been living for seven years, fearing Parker's release. You sent a man to break into my house in Los Angeles to see how much I knew about you and, I assume, your connection to Parker. You can act indignant, you can pretend to be shocked by all of this, but you're not convincing me, and you need me on your side. This will all get ugly if you try to work things out on your own. Trust me. I'm the best friend you've got right now."

Soledad laughed. "Scotty once told me if anyone ever says, 'Trust me. I'm the best friend you've got right now,' I should run from that person as fast and as far as I could."

"You might want to think through that advice," I said, "given the circumstances."

She studied my face. "You have his eyes."

"Miss Varela ..."

"I don't think he intended for this to happen. For us to ever meet."

"And yet here we are. Can we stay on topic?"

When she spoke again, her voice grew soft and fragile. "He was so proud of you. He talked about it often. He said you were a much better cop than he was, and that was the one good thing he could leave behind."

My emotions roiled, hearing this. It was her intention, I'm sure—to play to my heart and my love for my father. To exploit the loss still filling me and unnerve me. I glanced at Charley and saw equal skepticism in her eyes.

"Did he ever mention me to you?" Soledad asked.

"No."

"I imagine he was ashamed."

She sank down into a chair, raising a hand to her neck and massaging it. She eyed the shoebox on the coffee table containing our father's badge, his medals, and the gun that killed him. I picked up the box and moved it out of her reach, putting it on a shelf by the front door.

"It was a stupid thing, my getting involved with Colin Parker," she said. "I was young, naïve. And I guess part of me resented Scotty, even though he was helping me out after my mother died. He'd had it good, never having to worry about me, while I grew up in the household of a monster."

"Carlos Varela went to jail before you were born."

"Not him," she said. "My mother. You have no idea what she was like. Vicious. Hateful toward me. She was free of Carlos, only to be saddled with a child she didn't expect or want. It infuriated her. Especially when the money ran out."

"So she came to Scotty for help."

"Of course. Wouldn't you? She played him, filled him with guilt, to get what she wanted."

"I'm surprised it worked," I said. "He had no reason to feel guilty. He had no idea you even existed. And once he did, he helped out."

"That was Scotty's flaw. He was too good. I think he carried guilt that went far back. I was the proverbial straw that broke his back."

"Your attempt at insight into a man you barely knew is admirable," I said.

Charley jumped in, sensing that, despite my best intentions to stay on track, I could easily be pulled into a fight to defend my dad. "You were telling us why you got involved with Colin Parker," she said.

Soledad shot her a disdainful look, but said, "I did it to make Scotty crazy. He considered Colin the most dangerous of his crew."

"Why?" I asked.

"Colin was a psychopath. And obviously still is. He fell in love with me, but I only used him to hurt Scotty."

"You never had honest feelings for him?"

"Of course not." She lowered her eyes as she spoke, indicating a lie. "I can't tell you how relieved I felt after they'd sentenced him and carted him off to jail."

"Dad sent Parker to jail to keep him away from you. He must have sensed something that made him think he needed to keep you two apart."

Soledad paused. "I've made many mistakes. You never can really leave them behind." Tears sprung in her eyes. She had loved Parker, I could tell, even if she now feared him.

"Where is he, Soledad?"

She slumped back. "Out at your father's cabin, in Goleta. He attacked me there earlier. I shot him. It was self-defense. I was scared for my life. He may be dead. I don't know. I didn't wait around."

29

S
he had re-locked the shed door before departing, but it was made of thin wood. With three well-placed kicks, Trane broke it in, forcing it against its hinges, the screws pulling loose from the doorpost with a screech. He felt hot and feverish, sweat causing his shirt to cling to his skin, and the comforting cool inside was like walking into a large icebox. Despite this, the wound on his upper arm burned like a branding iron had been slapped against the skin.

It took a few seconds for his eyes to adjust to the darkness. When they did, he saw a normal-looking shed filled with typical gardening equipment: tools hung on the walls, bags of fertilizer piled along the back, a small riding lawnmower parked in a corner. Most boxes on the bookcase contained metal watering cans and packets of plant food—but one shelf held a black duffel bag. He reached up with his good arm, took down the bag, and unzipped it to reveal dozens of packets of twenty-dollar bills. He rifled through them, doing quick calculations in his head.

Barely a hundred thousand.

Jesus. All this for a hundred grand?

He thought of a line from an old noir film he liked about killing for money and a woman but not getting the money and not getting the woman. With the thought, his dizziness returned. He had to steady himself by leaning against the worktable. The pain from the gunshot was almost unbearable. He zipped the bag back up and staggered out into bright sunshine that blinded him, tossed the duffel onto the backseat of his car, then went inside the cabin.

In the bathroom, Trane found Advil, gauze, and surgical tape. He stripped off his jacket and shirt, then doused a small knife and pair of tongs he'd taken from a kitchen drawer with rubbing alcohol. Sitting on the closed toilet lid, waiting for the effects of the four Advil he had downed with some bourbon, he found his thoughts returned to Soledad. He had imagined many reactions from her but never one in which she'd shoot to kill. The look in her eyes today was not fear but hatred.

Damn you, Scotty. You've ruined even this part of my life.

When the pills brought his pain down to a dull throb, he poured rubbing alcohol over the bullet wound. The sting was intense, despite the painkillers. Using the kitchen knife, he widened the hole in his arm, then—with the help of a tabletop mirror—he dug in with the tongs, pushing them as deep as they would go, trying to grab the bullet. He bit down on the handle of the knife. His heart pounded, feeling like it might push right out of his chest. Vomit surged up into the back of his throat, and he forced it down. Finally, he pulled the smashed metal slug out of the wound and dropped it into the sink.

After rinsing his arm once more with alcohol and water, he used a sewing needle and some thread to stitch himself up. He pierced his skin and drew the filament across the gaping hole, again and again, until he reached the other side. He knotted the string, cut the needle loose, then covered the suture with gauze and surgical tape.

In a trunk in the main bedroom closet he found men's clothing: a white T-shirt, a light blue Oxford, and faded jeans. The clothes, either Jason's or Scotty's, smelled of mothballs and that peculiar hint of dry-cleaning gasoline. It hurt to pull the shirtsleeve up his wounded arm and to get into the jeans. Dressing took him a good five minutes. Everything fit loosely on his thin frame, but at least it was clean and didn't stink of sweat and blood. He tossed his dirty clothes onto the floor, down with the mess he'd made during his earlier search. It didn't concern him. He planned on burning this house down too.

The sound of a car, approaching up the front drive, cut through the silence. Soledad returning? A change of heart? Or was she back to make sure she had killed him?

He went into the living room and glanced out the front window. Three vehicles were parked in the driveway: a black Jeep Wrangler, a local police cruiser, and a dark-blue, older-model Crown Victoria. Jason Chance and a woman Trane recognized as Charlotte Frasier were just getting out of the Jeep. A slender woman in a black skirt suit and orange shirt stood beside the sedan with two uniformed officers.

Why the hell had they come here? Had Soledad sent them? Or was this just a bad coincidence?

Whatever the reason, he had no choice but to kill them all.

I FELT A SENSE OF DÉJÀ VU LOOKING AT THE CABIN, AS IF WE'D never left. I glanced over at Charley.

"Weird, huh," she said.

I nodded and took my keychain from my pocket. I hadn't removed the cabin key from the ring yet.

"So where's this body supposed to be?" Detective Downs said.

"Around back," I said. "That's where Soledad said she left him."

The detective nodded and headed for side of the house, motioning for the officers to follow.

Charley said, "You know there's every chance this is one big trap."

"It crossed my mind."

"We might want to think about going in with something more than our winning personalities."

"Good point." I went back to the Jeep and reached in to open the glove compartment and take out my handgun. "Better?"

Charley nodded. I clipped the holster to my belt and removed the pistol as we stepped up to the front door. I unlocked it and eased it open. The living room was a mess, torn apart by an extensive search. Soledad told us she had never entered the cabin but had gone straight to the backyard, where Parker attacked her. She wouldn't tell us why she had come here or what she was after, claiming it was private and personal, none of our business. I had my suspicions: Petrov's money. According to Soledad, Parker came at her from the kitchen door. This meant he had somehow gained access to the cabin. He hadn't tampered with the front door, and the alarm was disarmed. He must have a duplicate key, along with the security system code, most likely taken from Evelyn before he strangled her to death.

Charley stepped toward the archway that led to the kitchen. "You smell that?"

I stopped and inhaled, picking up the odor of gas mixed with burning paper.

"We shut everything off before we left, right?" I said.

"I checked twice."

Gunfire then *boomed* from the backyard, three blasts in sequence, followed by silence. No return fire. I had an immediate, sickly feeling. I motioned for Charley to get away from the archway, thinking Parker would come at us through the kitchen door, but before she could make a move or even acknowledge my command, the back of the house exploded in a fireball. The blast threw me back against the sofa with such force it toppled over. My head and back slammed down on the hardwood floor. An overwhelming heat flooded past me. I tried to call Charley's name, but the impact had knocked the wind out of me. I rolled on my side, still unable to breathe, and scanned the room for her location. I saw only fire and billowing smoke.

It took a few more seconds for my diaphragm to relax, allowing me to gulp in air. My lungs filled with more smoke than oxygen. I coughed and spat, trying to get to my feet. My eyes stung. I felt a sharp pain in my leg. Looking down, I saw a chunk of wood from a splintered two-by-four embedded in my thigh. A circle of blood spread out from it, growing larger.

I sat back and grabbed hold of the stake. As I yanked out, a geyser of blood shot up through the smoke. Everything inside my head went lopsided, and I fell over, puking out a stream of bile. I undid my belt buckle and jerked it loose from my pants, then wrapped the leather around my thigh, just above the wound, and cinched it as tightly as I could stand.

"Charley," I called, my shout prompting another coughing fit. "Charley, can you hear me?"

She choked out a cry from a corner of the room. Not since hearing the first wails of the newborn Kathy had I been more grateful for a sound of life. Struggling to my feet, I covered my mouth and nose with the crook of my elbow and moved toward the corner. Smoke and flames engulfed the back half of the house now, consuming the walls at a fierce rate, eating through the division between the kitchen and the living room. We had minutes before it also devoured us.

Charley lay sprawled on her belly. I stumbled over, knelt down, and gently turned her over. Her face and neck were red, black, and blistered. Her left pant leg was on fire from the ankle to the knee. I pulled off my shirt and used it to blot out the flames, then scooped her into my arms and stood. I felt disoriented and weak, overwhelmed by the heat and the smoke.

I carried her toward the front of the house, trying to stay ahead of the spreading inferno. Six feet from the door, a side wall collapsed and sent a burning beam of wood crashing down in front of us, blocking our path. Its tip landed on the sofa. Within seconds, the fabric was ablaze. Burning chips of wood and plasterboard flew around me like confetti. The smoke was intense, and the lack of breathable air made me lightheaded. My hold on Charley weakened. The pain flared in my leg with every step. I screamed, a wail of exasperation, and sprinted for the side window, our only chance of escape.

30

I set Charley down in an armchair, its high back protecting her from the approaching flames, then I grabbed up the small end table beside it and used it to smash through the glass of the side window. Then I pushed out the remaining shards. Scooping Charley back up into my arms, I eased her through the opening and lowered her to the ground outside.

I could feel the heat of the fire getting closer as I hoisted myself up and jumped out, landing on my haunches in the grass. I gulped in fresh air. Looking over, I saw the blaze eating through the cabin wall. Soon, it would burst out in a mass of flames. I rushed away from the building with Charley in my arms just as a spray of fire shot out through the window opening. She cried out, looking around, terrified.

"We're out," I said. "We're okay."

With weak breath, she whispered, "Can't take the pain."

"I know. I'm going to get you to the hospital."

In the sunlight, I saw the extent of her injuries. The fabric of her shirt on the left arm was burned away, the skin underneath it red and bubbling with pus. The burns extended up her shoulder and neck onto her cheek. Her lips were blistered and swollen. Small chips of wood from the explosion were embedded in her forehead. Blood, still moist and fresh, dripped into her eyes.

I carried her to my Jeep in the front of the building and laid her down on the backseat. I could hear sirens in the distance. Someone in a nearby home, or a driver down on the road, must have seen the fire and smoke and called it in. There was little chance they'd be able to save the cabin— the flames, now towering a good ten feet into the air, had engulfed the entire structure—but at least they could stop the blaze from spreading to the woods.

"I've got to check on the detective and the officers," I said. "Try not to move. I'll be right back."

Charley nodded and closed her eyes. I slammed shut the car door, and then hobbled around to the rear of the house, the pain in my leg now almost unbearable. Rounding the back corner, I spotted Detective Downs first. She lay face up near the shed, a bullet wound in her forehead. The officers were sprawled side by side a few feet away, both on their stomachs, circles of blood covering each one's shirt like bull's-eyes. None of them had even the chance to draw their weapons. Parker had ambushed and shot them in rapid sequence.

A DOCTOR AT GOLETA VALLEY COTTAGE HOSPITAL EXAMINED Charley, evaluating the extent of her burns and smoke inhalation, while a nurse cleaned and stitched my leg wound. He gave me antibiotics and some painkillers (which I pocketed, needing a clear mind).

"My name is Jason Chance," I told the nurse. "I'm a

homicide detective with the Los Angeles Sheriff's Department. I need you to do something for me. Keep it quiet that we came in. Someone may call or come by asking about burn patients. They might even ask for me or Charlotte Frasier by name. They cannot under any circumstances know we're here. It's a matter of life and death. Do you understand?"

"Got it," the nurse said. "You were never here. I'll let everyone know we should not tell anyone."

I thanked him, and he left. I waited in the empty cubicle, an oxygen tube in my nose, and tried not to worry about Charley by focusing on Colin Parker. Where would he head? Would he try to go after Soledad? Or would he just disappear?

Charley's doctor came in thirty minutes later and give me the lowdown. "She's got first- and second-degree burns on her torso, left arm, neck, and half her face. We've cleaned and dressed the wounds and put her on antibiotics. I want to keep her overnight to monitor for infection and dehydration."

"Can I see her?" I asked.

"She's sedated and won't be very responsive."

"I don't care. I just want to sit with her."

The doctor led me to her cubicle, and then left us alone. They'd stripped her of her burned, soot-covered clothes, and a sheet covered her abdomen and legs. Her torso, arm, and shoulder were bandaged with moist gauze. An IV jutted out of her right hand, its tube attached to a bag of clear liquid on a stand. Another tube looped across her upper lip, like the one I'd had, giving her fresh oxygen. A monitor above her head displayed her vital signs. Everything looked steady and strong.

"Jagger," she whispered, attempting a smile.

"Shh, don't talk. Go back to sleep."

"Can't. Pain's too strong."

"That'll ease up soon," I said, though I had no idea if this was true.

"Detective Downs?"

"Dead. The officers too."

"What about Parker?"

"Forget him. Right now, what matters is you."

"He'll run. Disappear. Not much time …"

"I'm not going anywhere."

"Jagger, you have to. What are you going to do here? Nothing. He's not going to come back. He has no reason to take the chance. He's on the run. Go get him. Do it for me."

TRANE SLAMMED SHUT THE MOTEL-ROOM DOOR AND FLIPPED the security bar into place. He ripped off his shirt, then the bandage, and looked down at the wound. The stitches had come loose. Blood oozed down his arm. He couldn't waste time stitching it up again; he would re-bandage it, then get medical attention once he got someplace safe.

He was a mess all over. His head ached almost as much as the bullet wound. His heart beat in his chest like a derelict pounding on a door, screaming to get out. He grabbed a fifth of Johnny Black from his overnight bag and took a pull straight from the bottleneck. The scotch burned his throat as it went down.

Nothing's ever as easy as you think it will be, is it? Even when you expect it's gonna be tough, it ends up worse.

Trane sat on the edge of the bed and chased down three more Advil with another long drink. As the booze went to work on him, his heart rate slowed, but his dark thoughts intensified. Everything had gone to hell. He'd been shot. He

was racking up a body count higher than he ever antici-
pated. What he'd hoped would have been a payday of
millions turned out to be less than a hundred thousand
bucks.

But Soledad's reaction to seeing him hit the hardest and
hurt the most. His journey was never about the money; that
was a means to a better end for them. This had always been
about her.

All that energy and love, wasted.

To top it all off, Jason and Charlotte escaped the blaze.
The fuckers got out. They survived. He only knew this
because he'd stayed at the highway to watch the flames, and
he saw Jason come down the driveway and head off in
his Jeep.

Trane moaned aloud, sounding like a wounded animal,
and threw the whisky bottle at the wall. It shattered, the
liquid dripping down like amber tears. He grabbed his
phone, opened his music app, and turned on Coltrane's
Giant Steps album. Stretching out on the bed, waiting for the
latest batch of painkillers to take effect, he closed his eyes
and let Coltrane's intricate sax playing go to work on his
brain. He often did this during times of stress. It was his
form of meditation. By the time "Spiral" came on, calmness
had taken hold, and he could think through his situation
and options.

He had to get more money; that was foremost. He
couldn't escape, couldn't even operate without it. The
measly hundred thou he'd found in the shed wouldn't last
six months, and he had already depleted most of the savings
he had put away before he went to prison. He needed a
fresh influx. But from where?

He thought about the information he'd learned from
Ziggy and Heather: the intel regarding Jensen Vanderbrook

and his missing son. Three million dollars offered. Money just waiting to be handed over to someone with something to offer. But how to get that something? Jason was probably the only one who knew the truth.

Trane did a Google search on his laptop of the nearest hospital to the cabin. Using a burner phone, he called the emergency room of Goleta Valley Cottage Hospital and identified himself as Captain Germaine Ellison. He gave a phony badge number and said he was checking nearby hospitals for one of his detectives, Jason Chance.

"I'm sorry. We're not at liberty to give out that information."

"I just need to know what his condition is."

"There have been no patients admitted under that name, sir. That's all I can tell you." The man ended the call, too abruptly for Trane to ignore. The man would have cooperated with a police officer unless he had been instructed not to.

Trane packed his overnight bag and loaded it into the car, then drove to a street behind the motel, parking so that his car was shielded from view by a large trash receptacle on one side and an overgrown bougainvillea bush on the other. It was late in the afternoon of a hot, lazy day; there wasn't much activity on the street. Taking a screwdriver from a tool kit in the trunk, he unscrewed the front and back license plates from his vehicle. Next, he removed the plates from a nearby BMW 328. Working quickly, he mounted the 328's plates onto his Beemer and his on the 328. No one watched him; no one noticed.

31

I stepped outside the ER and called Ellison to fill him in.

"From the sound of things, you got lucky," he said. "How bad off is Charley?"

"The burns are severe. They're keeping her overnight."

"I guess that means you're staying there too."

"No, there's little I can do here. I've put on a local cop to guard her hospital room." I watched an ambulance pull to a stop in front of the big ER doors. The paramedics unloaded a gurney with an elderly man who had an oxygen mask over his face and an IV in his forearm. They wheeled him inside.

"So what are you thinking?" Ellison asked.

"I need to figure out where Parker's heading. I'm hoping Soledad can point me in the right direction."

"Listen, Jay, there's something you need to know."

"Yeah?"

"We got an ID on the guy who tried to kill Paula Ramirez and probably was behind the Armando Trujillo assassination. The man's name is William Neiffer. Ex-Navy Seal. Been on the wrong side of things since he got back from Afghanistan in 2014. Mostly gun-for-hire stuff."

"I've never heard of him."

"You'd have had no reason to. It's not him you should worry about ..."

"But who hired him," I said.

"Right. That's the part you're not going to like. Fifty thousand dollars was direct-deposited into his account one week ago. We did a trace. The money was wired out of a Santa Barbara bank account in Scotty's name."

Once again, my father—it all kept coming back to him. And he was dead and couldn't have sent the cash to the killer, so it wasn't hard to figure out who had.

TRANE PULLED INTO THE HOSPITAL PARKING LOT AND EASED TO a stop beside a row of short palm trees where he had a straight view of the building through his windshield. The sky was creeping toward darkness, the electrical lights of the lot just turning on overhead. He spotted Jason pacing back and forth by the stucco portico that covered the emergency room drop-off door, talking on his cell phone. A limp to his walk and a dark stain around a tear in his jeans told Trane the detective had been injured in the explosion. What about Charley? Was she inside the ER? In worse condition? Was she even still alive? He hadn't seen her in the Jeep as Jason drove away from the burning cabin, but she could have been lying in the backseat. That they'd escaped at all amazed Trane.

Across the lot, Jason ended the phone call, slipped his cell into his back pocket, and walked over to his Wrangler. The roof and sides of the Jeep were dusted with gray ash flakes from the cabin fire. The detective backed the Wran-

"You don't really want to know the truth about your father. It terrifies you. And your confusion runs deeper. Trying to save our father's reputation is just an excuse. You're trying to hold onto something bigger and more important to you, but it's slipping away, isn't it?"

"I'm not sure I know what you mean."

"Yes, you do. I'm talking about your belief that any of this matters. You hope you can actually make a difference, but more times than not, you end up hurting the people you love in the process. And that haunts you."

I sat back, disturbed by how well she could read me. This couldn't simply be insight on her part. She had followed my actions, my career, wanting to know about a brother she could never approach.

"Did I hit a nerve?" she said.

"No," I said, although she had. "I'm just tired of dancing around this with you." I waited for her to say something, but she remained silent. I stood up. "I'm going to make some coffee. Want a cup?"

"Sure. Black."

I went into the kitchen, where I splashed my face with cold water and drank several handfuls. I wanted a beer, not coffee, or a drink of bourbon—anything that would calm my nerves. I opened the fridge but closed it again right away. That's when I noticed the photo of the young girl, maybe eight years old, stuck to the door with a magnet.

32

I t was a small hospital, with a reduced night staff and minimal security. This allowed Trane to slip easily past the triage station into the main emergency room area. A guard sat across from a cubicle Trane assumed held Charley Frasier. He went into a nearby empty one, pulled the curtain shut—leaving only enough of an opening to see the guard—and sat on the bed. *Just a guy with an injury waiting for a doctor to come and examine him.*

The sound of the car crash outside was loud and right on time. An exchange of gunfire followed. The guard across the aisle reacted as Trane hoped, jumping to his feet and hurrying over to the nurses' station to get a better view of the front of the emergency room and ascertain what had happened. He said something into the mic attached to his shirt's left shoulder strap.

Trane stepped out of the cubicle, removing a hypodermic syringe from his jacket pocket. He flicked off the plastic tip covering the needle as he came up behind the guard—who was telling his dispatcher that there had been some sort of crash outside followed by gunfire—and wrapped one arm around the man's torso while jamming the needle into his neck. The officer struggled for only a few seconds—the Etorphine dose was heavy—and soon, Trane felt the man go limp in his arms.

No one noticed. The doctor and nurses had all gone out front to investigate the parking lot incident. Trane dragged the unconscious police officer into the cubicle he had just vacated, laid him down on the bed and covered him with the sheet, then pulled shut the curtain as he exited again.

Charley lay on her back in the next cubicle, her upper body covered in gauze. Her eyes were closed. Trane found her belongings in a mesh bag hanging on the side of the bed and removed her wallet and cell phone. He used a second hypodermic to inject a smaller dose of Etorphine into her IV. Once he was sure the fast-acting drug had taken effect, he unplugged her heart and BP monitors and lifted Charley into his arms.

He carried her down a corridor and through a back exit that led to the small employee lot where he had parked his car. He placed her in the trunk, put her thumb against the home button of her phone to access it, then slammed closed the trunk lid, and got into the driver's seat. As he drove away, he flipped through her contacts until he found Jason Chance's number.

"Who's the little girl?" I asked Soledad, returning to the living room, holding the photo in my hand.

"That's none of your business," she said.

"Your daughter? Parker's daughter?" If the girl was the age she appeared in the photo, it wasn't hard to do the math.

"Give me that." Soledad stepped toward me, holding out her hand. I let her take the picture.

"Seems we're both trying to protect someone we care about," I said.

"You know nothing." She put the photo in her pocket.

My cell phone buzzed. Charley's name appeared on the screen as the incoming caller.

"Charley?" I said, answering. "What's wrong?"

"Hello, Jason." It was a man's voice, vaguely familiar. "Been a while, hasn't it?"

"Who are you? Where's Charlotte Frasier?"

"I'll give you a second to figure that out."

My stomach tightened. "Where is she, Parker? What have you done?" I looked over at Soledad. She'd stepped around behind the armchair and was staring back at me, her face rigid with what I could only gather was fear at hearing me say Parker's name.

"She'll be okay," Parker said to me, "as long as you play this smart. Is Soledad with you?"

"What does she have to do with this?"

"I'll take that as a yes. Meet me in Mojave. Highway 58. Drive east of the main town. There's an abandoned gasoline station about a mile and half out. You can't miss it. There's nothing else around. Come at 7 a.m., so the sun is up. Just you and Soledad. It's in the middle of nowhere, wide open views in every direction. I'll know if you've brought anyone else. Try to fuck me, Jason, and Charley dies." Parker didn't wait for me to respond. He ended the call.

"What did he want?" Soledad said.

"Nothing that concerns you."

"That's a lie. What did he say?"

I debated telling her the truth. Then the door opened, and the officers entered, returning from their search of Soledad's car. "It's clean," one of them said.

"Change of plans," I said. "Take Miss Varela into

custody." One asked what the charge should be. "Whatever you can make stick for twelve hours."

"What's going on?" Soledad said. "What did Parker want?"

"Take her," I told the cops.

As the officers stepped toward her, Soledad reached down under the cushion of the chair in front of her and snatched up my father's handgun. She must have gotten it from the drawer while I was in the kitchen. I'd let her get under my skin, taken my eye off the ball, and given her the upper hand. Three stupid clichés at once—how much dumber and more foolish could I have been?

33

"**D**on't be stupid," I said to Soledad. "You don't want to do this."

"What did Parker say?" Soledad demanded, ignoring my warning. "He told you where to meet him, didn't he? And he wants you to bring me."

"You're just making matters worse," I said. "Put the gun down, and we'll talk."

"No." I saw in her eyes the same scared, desperate gaze I've seen criminals get when they're cornered and about to make a wrongheaded decision. "You'll do as he told you," she said and raised her other hand to steady the gun. "You're taking me to him."

Trane pulled into the empty parking lot of a small mall outside Castaic Junction and parked in a far corner, away from the street. The stores were not yet open, and there were no other cars in the lot. The overhead halide lamps gave a glow to the fine morning mist.

He prepared another injection of the Etorphine, just

enough to keep Charley docile until they reached Mojave. He didn't have much more of the drug, so he needed to space out the doses to maintain control over her until the entire transaction was over, and she was no longer any use to him. At the rear of the car, he opened the trunk. Charley remained unconscious. The bandages on her upper torso had come loose during the abduction and ride, and in the harsh light, he saw more clearly the severity of her burns: red, twisted flesh across her chest and up onto her face. It looked grotesque.

Poor thing, he thought, injecting her in the neck with the opioid. *She'll need a lot of treatment and skin grafting to erase those injuries.* His empathy was sincere. He felt no hatred toward the woman. Hell, he barely knew her. Their paths had crossed a few times back when Scotty was alive, and Jason and she were living together. She struck Trane as a smart, serious person. But empathy could play no part in what Trane needed to do. Charley was a prop to him now. His leverage. He wouldn't think twice about killing her if it came to that. Her fate was in Jason Chance's hands.

Back on the road, Trane drove east, heading through dark forest with no street lights to guide the way, only blackness, headlight beams, and endless highway. He felt positive, back in control. A bad situation had been swept away like dirt out the door, and a better opportunity had presented itself. On the radio, Monk's "Bemsha Swing" matched Trane's upbeat mood.

As for Soledad, he hadn't yet figured out that part. He might forgive her if she convinced him she deserved it. If she even wanted that. Cornered, she would probably say anything to save her own life. He needed to look in her eyes. Then he could tell. He'd see the truth in them. If there was honesty, he would embrace her. If not, he would shoot her in the head. But he would kill her at last.

"THIS IS A FOOLISH MOVE, SOLEDAD," I SAID. "YOU'RE putting yourself and Charley in more danger." I'd her that Parker had Charley and was using her as leverage. "Let me deal with Parker on my own."

"He'll kill you, then Charley if I don't show up with you."

"And he'll probably kill you if I do. You shot him, intending to kill him. He's most likely out for blood. I don't want your death on my hands any more than I want Charley's. I have a better chance of surprise if I go in alone."

"Don't underestimate him, Jason. This is his métier. The art of the clandestine move. I can talk to him. I know him better than you do."

Soledad's argument made sense, but I didn't believe she actually planned to attempt to talk him down. I think she intended to kill him the moment she had the opportunity.

"I need to verify he's even got Charley," I said, "and that it isn't all a bluff." I didn't wait for her to respond. I took out my cell and called the police officer I had assigned to guard the hospital. He sounded groggy when he answered. I identified myself.

"I'm sorry, detective," he said and told me what had gone down. "Someone came up behind me and injected me with something. I never saw him coming. Miss Frasier is gone."

"How long ago did they leave?" I asked.

"I wasn't out more than half an hour."

"Check the hospital security recordings, see if there's any footage of the abduction. I want to know what car he's driving. Call me back at this number when you have information." I ended the call. "If we're going, we need to go now," I told Soledad, reversing my position.

Still holding the gun, she forced the officers to cuff themselves to the bedroom and bathroom doorknobs, leaving them with their cell phones—at my insistence—so they could call for help once we were gone. We left the apartment and went down to my Jeep. It was 3 a.m., and the streets around her building were quiet and deserted.

"He didn't mention the money," I said. "I'd thought he would've make sure that was part of the deal."

"Maybe he's accepted I don't have it," she said. "I wish everybody would."

"Parker killed eight people to find you and five million dollars. I doubt he's going to forget about it just because you told him to."

"No," she said, "you're probably right." She sounded exhausted. "And he's not Colin Parker anymore. He's *Trane* now, one hundred percent. The undercover psychopath." She looked straight into my eyes. "You have no idea what you're about to face."

We drove through the endless suburban tract houses that lined the Santa Paula Freeway through Ventura, most dark in the early morning hours. Soledad stayed quiet in the backseat and didn't argue when I put on Arcade Fire's *Everything Now* album. I turned it low and contacted Ellison for the fifth or sixth or seventh time. I'd lost count.

"He picked one hell of an out-of-the-way place to meet," Ellison said after I filled him in.

"I'll say."

"Any idea why?"

"All I can think is Mojave's not far from the California State Correctional Institute at Tehachapi. That's where Parker and Alex served their seven years. Hard to believe it's a coincidence."

"Probably not," Ellison said. "And there's an airport in Mojave. I'll find out which guards or other personnel had the most repeat contact with him. There might be a deal in play, some exit strategy."

"Anyone Parker set up to help him is going to expect a

Trane checked into a room on the first floor of the Desert Rose Motel in Mojave. He paid cash for two nights and got the key from a middle-aged, hippie-looking clerk, who seemed stoned and barely looked at him during the transaction. Trane then backed the Beemer into the parking space directly in front of the room so that the trunk faced the door. Only two other cars were parked in the lot, and the windows of all the rooms were dark.

Trane unlocked the room door and left it open, then popped the car trunk, and quickly carried Charley inside. He slammed the door shut with his foot. She remained unconscious as he laid her down on one of the two double beds and cuffed her right hand to the shaft of a lamp firmly bolted to the nightstand. He tested its sturdiness with a few strong tugs. Pus oozed from the blisters across Charley's neck and shoulder. Trane covered her with a sheet, so he wouldn't have to look at the disgusting sight.

He went back outside and retrieved a small suitcase from the car, closed and locked up the vehicle, then put the

"Do Not Disturb" sign on the door and locked it from inside, swinging the security bar into place. He set the suitcase down on the round table near the window. Inside were weapons he had purchased from a friend of the Tehachapi guards who would be helping him get out of the country: a Beretta 9mm, a .357 magnum revolver, and a Mac II subcompact machine pistol—the latter in case Chance decided to be ballsy and come in with a small army.

It was 5:30 a.m. The sun would be up in approximately one hour. Chance and Soledad should be arriving soon—*if* they followed orders. Trane pulled the curtains shut and turned on a floor lamp. From the top section of the suitcase, he removed several boxes of ammo and began loading the weapons.

ELLISON WAITED WHERE HE TOLD ME HE WOULD IN THE parking lot of Dale's Hardware, sitting behind the wheel of a dark-green Lincoln Town Car that looked as if it had traveled a hundred thousand miles. A half-dozen yards away, out of the light pool cast by a high lamp, I saw an LA Sheriff's Department cruiser with two deputies inside. I pulled to a stop next to Ellison's car. On the highway, Vanderbrook's black SUV drove past.

"Okay," I said, "we don't have a lot of time." I shifted in my seat, so I could face Soledad. "I know you're thinking that all we have to do is follow Trane's orders, show up where he tells us to go, and then you'll kill him before he can stop you."

"That's a hell of a presumption."

"Don't waste time denying it. My point is: it won't work. That's not going to be the plan. Here's what will probably happen if we do as he tells us. We'll walk into an empty garage. He'll be in another location altogether but close. He'll have a camera or some sort of monitoring device in place, so he can see us arrive." Behind me, Ellison tapped on my car window. I raised a finger for him to give us a moment.

"Once we're in the location, I'll get a phone call with instructions. He'll tell me where to go to find Charley, and he'll want you to stay behind in the garage. I'll demand Trane let me speak with her. She'll still be alive for that sole reason, and he'll kill her the minute I end the call." Soledad fidgeted in her seat. "I'll be shot once I step out into the open. The one thing I can't predict is what he plans to do with you."

Her hands and the gun they held trembled.

"You're scared, and I don't blame you," I said. "But if you trust me and do as I say, I may be able to keep us all from getting killed."

Her eyes grew red as they teared up. Once again, she'd dropped the mask of strength and let me see a moment of true emotion.

"Will you do that? Will you trust me and let me take the reins here?" I asked.

Soledad nodded, then took hold of the gun barrel with her free hand and turned it so I could take the grip. I stored my father's pistol in the glove compartment. "He won't let you take him alive, you know," she said.

"We'll see," I said, opening the door. I greeted Ellison and introduced him to my half-sister.

CHARLEY MOANED AS THE ETORPHINE IN HER SYSTEM WORE off. Trane looked up from his work. With consciousness, the pain returned, and she cried out, wildness mixed with confusion filling her eyes. She pulled against the cuff. Realizing she was trapped, she screamed out, "Help! Help me, somebody!" She turned to look at the phone, read the room number on it, then shouted, "I'm in room 214! I'm being held against my will. Somebody, please!"

Trane let her shout. He'd rented out the rooms on either side, as well as the one directly above them. There was no one to hear her cries.

"Help me!" she cried. "Room 214!"

Trane picked up another syringe from the table. This was the last dose he had, so he'd give her only half. Enough to sedate her but not completely knock her out. He needed her conscious to speak when Chance inevitably asked for proof of life. Trane clamped his free hand down over her mouth, at the same time flicking off the plastic tip covering the needle with his other thumb. Charley bit into his palm with such force that she broke the skin.

"Fuck!" He pulled his hand away and looked at the wound to see how bad it was.

Charley doubled her legs, bending them until her knees touched her chest while shifting her body to the right, and kicked out. The soles of her feet slammed into Trane's chest. The move caught him off guard—she was quicker and stronger than he expected. He staggered back, dropping the syringe to the floor. Charley kicked again. This time, her foot smashed into his chin. The blow knocked him over.

"Help me!" she screamed.

"No one can hear you, ya stupid cunt!" Trane grabbed the fallen syringe and got to his feet. He moved back toward the bed, putting the hypo between his teeth while bobbing out of the way of her lashing legs. He grabbed her ankles and forced them down to the bed, so he could sit on them.

"I'm going to enjoy killing you," he said and punched her in the face.

The blow stunned her and slowed her movements, allowing him to jam the tip of the syringe into her thigh. He injected a quarter of its contents into her body, staying on top of her as she wiggled and struggled until the drug took effect. Once it did, her spasms eased, and her eyes fluttered, then closed. He could feel her body relax beneath him.

Trane stood and went into the bathroom. He washed his hand, repeatedly soaping and rinsing the wound. Her bite had gone deep. And, of course, it *would* be on the same side as the gunshot wound. He had no gauze left, so he tore a towel into strips and wrapped one tightly around his palm.

In the bedroom, Charley's breaths came slow and smooth. Her eyes were half open, watching him as he entered from the bathroom and crossed to the window. She tried to say something, but the drug had made her jaw weak, and her tongue heavy.

Trane peeked through the curtains. Outside, the rising sun glowed across the desert horizon to the east. He took out his own phone and called up a surveillance app. He tapped a few icons, and the exterior of an old gas station and repair garage appeared on the small screen. He scrolled through several shots showing different angles of the structure, inside and out, as well as views of the desert landscape in all directions. A single car approached down the highway. Returning to the first image, Trane watched as Jason's black Jeep arrived at the station and pulled into the lot.

36

The sun was just rising above a distant range of low mountains, the sky a soft white turning to pale blue, as I parked my Jeep in the lot of the abandoned gas station. I walked to the edge of the highway and looked around in all directions. Trane was right; open desert surrounded the building on every side. Any approach in daylight would be seen—if you had surveillance on the landscape. Trane must have posted cameras. He had worked fast, too, setting all this up. Things had not gone as planned for him. He was improvising now, working on instinct. I could only hope that would make him careless.

I came to the destination alone. Soledad had acquiesced and agreed to stay with Ellison and his deputies. I had my gun in its holster, clipped to my belt in the small of my back, plus Soledad's handgun—my father's old service pistol—in my jacket pocket. The Jeep's headlights illuminated the dark interior of the station's front room. I saw no movement inside.

I approached the main glass doors, pulled them open, and stepped into a small space that had once housed a cashier's station and a wall of glass-fronted refrigerators, now empty. The moment the doors swung closed behind me, my phone rang.

Trane watched on his phone screen as Chance answered the call from his burner.

"I'm here," Jason said. "Now what?"

"Is Soledad with you?"

"You know she's not. You're watching the place. She's nearby, waiting to hear from me."

"That wasn't the plan," Trane said, sounding angry for effect, though he wasn't surprised. He had expected Chance to veer from the arrangement.

"I'm not going to walk into an ambush," Jason said. "Give me a little credit. Now I need to know Charley's alive."

"Of course." Trane stepped over to the bed. "She's a little out of it, I'm afraid." He slapped Charley's cheek until she opened her eyes. "Jason wants to know you're okay," he said, then put the phone on speaker and moved it close to Charley's mouth. "Talk to him, so we can conclude our business, and everyone goes home happy."

"Jason?" Charley said.

"Yes, it's me. How are you holding up?"

"Groggy, some kind of drug." She sounded like someone had taken hold of her tongue with a pair of pliers.

"Do you know where you are?"

Trane ended the call before she could say another word. "That'll do," he told Charley, then jammed the hypodermic into her leg, injecting the rest of the Etorphine into her veins. Her eyes fluttered then closed.

Trane called Jason again, taking the burner off speaker

and putting it to his ear. "Satisfied?" he said. "Now, here's what's going to happen—"

"No," Jason said, cutting him off. "I'm going to tell you what's going to happen. You give me Charley's location. Once I have her, and I see she's okay, I'll tell you where to find Soledad. That's the only way you're going to get close to my sister. And it's the only way you're going to get your money."

With this final statement, Jason showed Trane his hand. Soledad's claim that she didn't have Petrov's millions had been one of the few things she said to him that he believed —which meant this was a bluff. Jason also had to know there was no money. He was simply using Soledad as bait. Trane wondered if he'd forced her into this situation, or she'd come along willingly.

"Soledad doesn't have the money," Trane said. "You and I both know it, but I no longer care about that. I've made other arrangements."

"What arrangements?"

"You're about to have a visitor," Trane said. "Give him what he wants, and I won't kill Charley."

I ENTERED THE GARAGE AND SCANNED IT FOR THE HIDDEN camera, finally spotting a cell phone duct-taped to a pipe high on the ceiling. Parker must have downloaded some app that allowed one phone to work as a camera and the other as a monitor. Another cheap phone was taped to the wall in a corner. Outside, I found more phones placed on the east and west sides of the station.

A car approached on the highway. I took out my cell and sent Ellison a quick text with the phone number Trane had last used to call me. When the black SUV reached the station, it turned into the lot and pulled to a stop beside my Jeep. The back door opened. Jensen Vanderbrook exited the vehicle. Andre, his bodyguard, stayed by the driver's door.

"You don't seem surprised to see me," Vanderbrook said.

"I spotted your car in Palmdale," I said.

"I suspected you might. Should we talk inside?"

"I'd rather stay out in the open," I said.

Vanderbrook chuckled, but it was hollow, void of any real humor. "I'm not here to kill you, detective. Quite the contrary. We can do each other a favor."

"Is that what Colin Parker told you?"

Vanderbrook sighed. "Andre, would you take the guns from Mr. Chance, please? I'd hate for any accidents to happen in the heat of the moment."

Andre came over and patted me down. He took the gun from my holster and the other from my jacket pocket.

"How much are you paying Colin Parker for me to give you information?" I said. "The three million you offered the public? Or did he raise the price? He'd been expecting a five-million-dollar payday when he got out of prison, but that didn't work out. It was a clever move on his part to turn to you."

"My arrangements with Mr. Parker are of no concern here. The only thing that should matter to you is Charlotte Frasier's safety."

"Charley's gonna be fine. So am I." From my pocket, I took a folded piece of paper, which I had asked Ellison to procure for me right after I spotted Vanderbrook's SUV. A flicker of doubt and confusion flashed in the billionaire's eyes. "This is a warrant to search your vehicle," I said, "where I suspect I will find a large sum of money in cash. Maybe three million. Maybe five million. Maybe more. The amount, as you say, doesn't matter. I've also got a warrant to check your cell phone, where I believe I'll find multiple communications with a phone we will later be able to connect to Colin Parker. All of this will be added to a case against you, along with a charge of collusion. You've made a deal with a murder suspect to extort information from a detective of the Los Angeles Sheriff's Department in exchange for the release of a hostage. Extortion and kidnapping are felonies under California penal code 518 PC and California penal code section 207."

"I think you'll be hard pressed to prove any of that," Vanderbrook said. "And it might cost your friend her life."

"That, sir, sounds like a threat."

"No, not at all. We're two men talking in the middle of the desert. There's no one else around, except Andre. And he'll say whatever I tell him to say."

"You came out here with false confidence, Mr. Vanderbrook. I'm sure Parker told you I'd play along, that I'd do anything to protect Charley. He was right. But here's the thing: Parker has no sympathy for your situation. He's simply using you. However, I understand where you're coming from. How this affects me is no longer important, so I've got a better deal to offer you."

Vanderbrook stared at me, squinting against the sun. "I'm listening."

37

The burner phone Trane had used to call Chance buzzed on the table. Trane didn't recognize the incoming number. He glanced over at Charley on the bed before answering. She remained semi-conscious, the strip of dark-gray duct tape he had placed across her mouth looking like a gaping wound.

"What?" he said into the phone.

"Colin? It's me."

Trane didn't need more identification. Her voice was enough. *Soledad*.

His chest tightened as it had in the cabin when he first saw her. A shiver ran up his arms. All his anger and disappointment fell away, and his mind filled with images of her eyes, her dark skin, her sad smile. All from just hearing her say his real name. "Hello, Soledad."

"Things certainly got messed up, didn't they?" she said. She sounded a million miles away. He hated that he wasn't able to see her.

"Yeah, they did." He paused, pushing the .357 and the

subcompact pistol away, so he could lean forward on the table. "Life is messy."

"Ours sure is."

"Where are you?"

"In a car somewhere in the desert."

"With Jason Chance?"

"No, I'm with an LA sheriff's captain named Ellison and two deputies."

"Have they arrested you?"

"I'm pretty much getting the silent treatment."

"Except to tell you to call me."

What is Chance's strategy? Trane wondered. *To confuse? Disorient? Or simply distract?* "Hold on a second," he said, then picked up his personal phone and looked at the screen, flicking through the various angles on the gas station, inside and out. Vanderbrook and his driver were getting into the SUV. There was no sign of Jason on any of the screens. His black Jeep was gone from the lot.

Trane returned to Soledad on the burner cell. "What are you supposed to tell me?" he asked.

"They want me to convince you to give up. They say they know where you are. They've been able to ping your phone. Deputies are on the way to the hotel now."

He ended the call and tossed the phone aside. *It's not possible*, he told himself. That she'd said *hotel* and not *motel* proved it was a ruse. From the weapons suitcase, he removed yet another burner. He had three fresh ones left. He called the number Soledad had just used.

"They're lying," he said to her. "You know that, right? You're a distraction for me while Jason attempts to figure out where I am. But it's too late. I've taken care of things, and I'm back in control. The only question left for me is you."

"Me? What does that mean?"

"It means I'm willing to give you another chance. Because I know there's a part of you that still loves me."

"What is it you want?" she asked.

"What I've wanted from the moment I stepped out of prison. To be with you. For the two of us to go away together."

"And then what? You killed a lot of people. We'd always be on the run."

"Three million dollars could buy us whole new lives."

"For the last time, there is no money. Why does everyone think I have it? Scotty gave me a half a million dollars two days before he killed himself. That's all. I kept it hidden in the shed at the cabin and took from it as I needed. It's been six years. Most of it is gone." Trane heard frustration in her voice and, beneath it, a hint of desperation.

"I'm not talking about the money from Scotty," Trane said. His previous burner phone, the one he had tossed to the side, beeped now with an incoming call. Vanderbrook. "I've made other arrangements. After today, we'll have plenty from another source."

"What arrangements?"

"Don't ask questions," Trane said. "Just tell me you love me. Tell me you'll go away with me. I'll make the rest happen."

"No. I won't. I can't." He now heard unmistakable finality in her tone. He didn't need to look in her eyes. He knew. It was over. Soledad was gone. Out of his life forever. The inevitability of time had cursed him.

Nothing is constant. Nothing remains the same.

"Then goodbye," he said and ended the call. He threw the phone at the wall in anger and frustration, the screen smashing on impact.

Charley moaned. Trane glared at her. He was tempted to

shoot her now. Just kill her and flee. Forget about Soledad and Vanderbrook's money. Run and never look back.

No, not without a payout. He couldn't walk away with nothing. Not after everything he'd been through and done.

He grabbed the buzzing burner and answered.

"It's me," Vanderbrook said. "Chance gave me what I wanted. And I have what we agreed on for you."

Trane looked at the surveillance app screen. Vanderbrook's SUV was still parked in the lot of the abandoned garage.

"Where's Chance?" Trane asked.

"I don't know. He took off. Said he wanted to be closer to town when you called to tell him where that woman was."

"Stay put," Trane said. "I'm on my way."

He checked Charley's handcuffs, then slapped a second strip of duct tape over the first on her mouth. He put the weapons back into the suitcase and closed the lid, turned off the lights, and left the motel room, leaving the "Do Not Disturb" sign in place.

The sun was painfully bright after the darkness of the motel room, and the desert heat was strong, even that early in the morning. The Beemer's interior already felt like an oven, the leather seat hot as he sat down on it. His shirt clung to his sweating skin. The wound on his arm and the bite on his hand ached.

Trane headed east on Highway 58, scheming out his next move. He'd also have to kill Vanderbrook and his driver. Bury them in the desert. *God, what a cluster-fuck.* But it was almost over. He was almost out of the woods.

He called Jason's cell phone. Chance answered without a greeting, simply saying, "I told Vanderbrook what he wanted to know."

"Good. Once I get what I want from him, we'll finish our business. Where are you now?"

"Parked in the lot of a doughnut shop in Mojave. Where's Charley?"

"I'll tell you once I have my money," Trane said. Chance had veered again from the plan just enough to make Trane angry. "Sit tight. Order some coffee, and wait. I'll call you soon."

As Trane approached the deserted gas station and garage, he scanned the landscape for Chance's Jeep. Still no sign of it. He pulled into the lot, parking beside the SUV.

Vanderbrook got out of the backseat but stayed standing by his vehicle. The driver remained behind the wheel. Trane got out and walked over to the billionaire. Seeing him in person, Trane was unimpressed. The man could've been anyone, were it not for his fortune. He'd simply had more luck and opportunity.

"Where is it?" Trane asked.

"In the back trunk," Vanderbrook said, nodding.

"What did you find out from Jason?"

"That my son is dead," Vanderbrook said.

"I'm sorry. Did Jason kill him?"

"He claims he didn't."

Trane chortled. "And you believed him?"

"Can we finish this? I need to get home."

"Don't we all?"

Trane strode past the burly man, toward the back of the SUV. He clutched the handle on the back door and turned it. The door swung out and up, revealing Jason inside, sitting on top of three black duffel bags, a gun in his hand.

38

Trane raised his hands and stepped back as I eased out of the rear of the SUV. "Well played, Jason," he said. "Knight takes bishop."

"And you're taking me to Charley," I said.

Trane didn't move. He looked down at the bags under my legs. "We had a deal. I thought you were a man of honor."

"Don't talk to me about honor. Back up. Keep your hands where I can see them."

Trane took two steps back. I slid out of the trunk of the SUV.

"You know the most important lesson I learned in prison?" Trane said, raising his hands by his face.

"I don't really care."

Trane ignored my comment. "It came from a life-timer who instructed me in the game of chess. 'Don't just keep your eyes on your opponents' immediate moves,' the old man said. 'Study the entire board. Anticipate.' That was my mistake here. I knew you'd try to fuck me. I just couldn't see the moves."

"Yeah, well, sorry to let you down," I said. "Come on."

"Am I free to go?" Vanderbrook said. "I have no stake in what happens next."

"No, you don't," I said. "But I'd like you to follow us back into town. Just in case something goes wrong on the drive."

"Fine," Vanderbrook said. "We'd be going that direction anyway." He reached over and slammed shut the rear door, then returned to his seat in the SUV.

I told Trane to get behind the wheel of his BMW, keeping the gun on him as I walked around to the passenger side.

"I'm curious. Where did you hide your car?" he asked, looking at me across the roof.

"I found a nice gulley, about three hundred yards behind the station," I pointed toward the back of the building with the thumb of my free hand. "One deep enough that you couldn't see it with your makeshift surveillance. I moved the Jeep while you were busy talking to Soledad."

Trane laughed and shook his head. "You think you cover all the angles, but you never can."

Beside us, Andre backed up the SUV, then drove over to the edge of the highway and stopped, waiting. Trane and I got into his BMW simultaneously. I held the gun low across my lap, the barrel aimed at his gut. I didn't risk trying to put on the seatbelt.

"It's my fault," he said. "Trying to get clever." He revved the engine several times. "I should've just stuck to a square trade: Soledad for Charley, even Steven, my love for yours. I had to get greedy."

"Just drive. Take me to her."

"Sure thing," he said and slammed his foot down on the accelerator. The car sped forward so quickly and abruptly that I had no time to brace for any impact. The hood slammed into the window of the gas station store, shattering the glass wall and sending me flying toward the dashboard. My head slammed into the wood trim above the glove compartment. With the impact, the gun dropped from my hand. Trane, who had been able to steady himself by gripping the steering wheel, turned in his seat and punched me in the face, hard, a direct hit to the nose. I felt cartilage and blood vessels break. Blood gushed down my lip. He hit me again, then a third time, knocking me senseless. The last thing I saw clearly was my blood on his knuckles.

I had only a vague sense of his right arm reaching across me to the door. I was able to clamp a hand on his wrist, but Trane had a better angle and more strength and easily shoved me off as he grabbed the door handle and pulled it up, opening the door. With his free hand, he gripped my shirt and shoved me toward the open door. My hands flailed around, trying to grab something to stop the fall. Trane slugged me one last time, and it was enough to finish the job.

I fell back, out of the car, landing on the hard surface of the lot. As Trane reached down for my gun on the floorboard, I spotted Andre standing behind him, outside the car. He fired a shot that shattered Trane's door window. The bullet missed Trane and chipped the dash. Trane put the car in reverse and stomped down on the accelerator. The car careened back, away from the station, reversing across the lot to the highway. Andre fired a second shot, and a headlight on the BMW exploded.

I got to my feet and pulled my second gun, my father's pistol—given back to me by Andre after Vanderbrook and I made our deal—and aimed at Trane's BMW as it sped off down the highway. I fired two shots, missing the car both times.

I ran past Andre, toward the SUV. I jumped behind the wheel.

"What the hell, Chance?" Vanderbrook said.

"Get out," I said.

TRANE FLOORED THE PEDAL AND GRIPPED THE WHEEL AS IF IT might fly loose. His whole body shook with violent tremors. He could hear only ringing in his ears, so loud it sounded like he had fallen into a pit of alarm clocks, all going off at once. In the rearview mirror, a tiny spot of black appeared in the distance behind him, growing in size as it gained speed and got closer. Vanderbrook's SUV, no doubt, with three million dollars in cash in the back. If Trane could outrace Jason and get back to the motel, this could still turn around. Trane still had Charley, the only leverage left.

TRANE HAD A SOLID LEAD OVER ME, BUT I HAD HIS MONEY IN the back of the SUV. Money the man would need if he had any lingering hope of getting away. Which meant Trane would bargain, and that would keep Charley alive.

I took out my cell and called him. "I've got what you want," I said. "Let's make a deal."

"I'd be hard pressed to trust anything you say right now, don't you think?"

"Why not? I want to keep Charley alive."

"Then why'd you fuck with the plan?"

"Your plan was to get the money, then kill Charley and me. You know it, and I know it. I'm doing everything I can to keep that from happening. I still think there can be a reasonable outcome to all this."

"I suspect your idea of reasonable is different from

mine." Trane went quiet for a moment, then said, "Stay on the line with me until we reach town. I don't want you calling Captain Ellison or anyone else."

"Deal," I said.

Parker went silent for a bit, then asked, "So what shall we discuss while we drive?"

"Talk to me about my father," I said.

"What?" Trane sounded genuinely surprised. "Why?"

"I want answers."

"What kind of answers? Do you want to hear me tell you he was a hero? The best damned lieutenant I ever worked for? A saint among men? Yeah, sure. He was all of those things."

"I want the truth." Around us, the empty desert gave way to business establishments and restaurants as we entered Mojave proper. Cars were out now. People walked around. The work day had begun. "How dirty was he? How deep in?"

"Why are you doing this, Jason?" Parker said. "What does it matter now? He's dead. Nobody's pointing fingers. 'Live with the successes,' Scotty always said. 'Forget the failures.' They don't matter in the grand scheme of things."

"They matter to me."

"Some of us are just born ugly. Live with it."

"How ugly was my old man?" I glanced down at the center console, only now noticing that Andre had left his cell phone there, connected to a USB port by a white cable.

"All right, fuck it," Trane said. "Why hold back? Scotty was as ugly as they come. And I've seen a lot. Going way back too. For every twenty percent we scammed or stole, your father took ten. We had to split the rest four ways. If any of us gave him shit, he'd play the Internal Affairs card."

"What about drugs?"

"Drugs, cash, he didn't care. Opportunity was opportunity."

I had suspected this, I had feared learning it from the start of this investigation, and I still wasn't prepared to hear it. "Did he ever murder anyone?"

"Three guys that I know of. One of them worked for Carlos Varela. He threatened to kill Soledad's mother, Leticia, on Carlos's orders, for sleeping with Scotty while Carlos was in prison. The assassin was looking for a payoff to keep his mouth shut. Scotty shot him in the head, dumped the body off Point Dume. Then, there was this piece of shit named Miller ..."

"That's enough. I don't need to hear about the other two."

"Now you're talking sensible," Trane said.

"Why didn't you bring him down with you when the hammer fell?"

"We couldn't. He never let evidence tie back to him. Nothing, I mean *nothing*, traced to Scotty. He was good that way. He kept dirt on all of us, though. His stay-out-of-jail package, he called it. Evidence of our crimes. He had us set up to take the fall if things ever went south. And in the end, he let us go down."

"Would you have nailed him if you could have?"

"The others, maybe. Alex, for sure. Not me."

"Why not?"

"As mad as I was, as much as I hated him at the end, I knew at least he'd take care of Soledad. Without him, she had no one. Nothing."

"He sent you to prison to keep you two apart."

"I know, and I get it. A father's instincts. Look, Jason, I'm a bastard. I don't deny that. But I loved her. You pick your battles, right?"

We'd reached a motel called The Desert Rose. Trane turned into the parking lot. I picked up Andre's phone, hoping it wasn't password protected. I lucked out.

"He did love you," Trane said to me. "And he was damned proud. It was important to him that you never find out what he really was. We all respected that."

I followed Trane into the lot and parked beside his wrecked car, quickly finishing a text on the other phone. I unplugged it, silenced it, and shoved it into my pocket. Then I picked up my father's gun from the passenger seat.

"So how do you want to play this?" he asked as I got out of the car. He had the gun he'd taken from me in his hand.

"Tell me where she is," I said. "I lock this car and go check on her. If she's okay, I'll toss you the keys, and you go your way."

"Why is it I doubt things will play out that smoothly?"

"I want her to be okay, Colin. That's all I care about. It's just me and you here."

"But I know your Captain Ellison is nearby. Soledad told me."

"That was just to rattle you and buy some time."

Trane smiled. "No, it wasn't." He shifted the gun from one hand to the other. His wounds were obviously hurting him. I probably could've taken him down right there, but for all I knew, he was lying about Charley, and she wasn't even here at the Desert Rose. "How about this scenario?" he said. "We go in together. You see she's okay. *Then* you give me the keys. *Then* I drive off into the sunset."

"I can live with that," I said. "Let's go."

39

I t hurt Trane to see the damage his escape had caused to the front of his beautiful car. But things get broken when your plans go awry. Little he could do about it. What mattered now was walking away intact.

Chance clicked a button on a key, and the lights of Vanderbrook's SUV flashed once, accompanied by a single *honk*, as he locked the car's doors. The detective had a gun in his other hand. Trane also had a firearm—the one he'd recovered when he threw Chance out of the car—but he had to hold it in his weaker hand because of the increasing pain all up and down his right arm from his gunshot wound and Charley's bite to his palm.

A motel guest exited a room at the end of the exterior corridor and headed for an adjacent diner. Chance and Trane both lowered their guns to their sides and watched as the man entered the restaurant.

"All right," Chance said. "Let's get this over with. Where is she?"

"Room 214," Trane said, nodding toward the door. They stepped onto the sidewalk of the first-floor porch that ran along the wall of motel room doors. "I never wanted it to come to this, Jason. I never wanted us to have to face off."

"No, you just wanted to kill anonymously while you searched for the location of a woman and a lot of money. You had no trouble slaughtering an innocent family."

"I don't expect you to understand," Trane said. "I'm not even sure I could explain it if I tried."

"Then do me a favor: don't try. Let's not talk about it. Let's just finish this."

"That's fine with me." Trane took out the room key from his jacket pocket and unlocked the door. "After you," he said, stepping aside so Chance could pass.

Scotty's son backed into the room, keeping his eyes and the gun on Trane. With the curtains closed, the room was dark, except for the irregular box of light the sunshine cast through the open door, across the carpet and the foot of the beds. Charley was on the far bed, as Trane had left her: still cuffed to the lamp, duct tape still covering her mouth. The Etorphine had worn off and her eyes were wide open. She looked at Trane, then over at Chance.

"Now, give me the keys to Vanderbrook's car," Trane said, "and we'll be done."

BEHIND TRANE, OUT IN THE LOT, I SAW ELLISON'S GREEN sedan pull up behind the SUV, blocking its exit. Next, a Los Angeles Sheriff's Department cruiser came to a stop beside it.

"You should put that away," I said. "There's been a change of plans."

Without lowering the weapon, Trane glanced over his shoulder as Ellison and two sheriff's deputies approached the door to the room.

"Drop the weapon, sir," one deputy called out.

"I guess this is checkmate," I said.

"I guess it is," Trane said. He dropped his left hand down to his side and stepped into the room, turning to face Ellison and the deputies as they entered.

"You okay, Jay?" Ellison asked.

"I've been better," I told him and went over to Charley. The burns were dark and blistering across her shoulder and up her neck. I gently pulled the duct tape off.

The first words out of her mouth were, "Get these fucking cuffs off me!" Her voice was hoarse and cracking but full of fire. I motioned for a deputy to come free her. His nametag read Johannsen. He approached, removed his key, and used it to un-cuff Charley. I gently rubbed her wrists, mindful of the burns.

"Put your gun down on the table," Ellison told Trane. "Nice and easy." Trane did as he was told, setting the gun down next to a small, closed suitcase. Ellison snatched up the weapon and handed it to the other deputy, an officer named Kelly. "Cuff him. Read him his rights."

Kelly walked toward Trane, taking a set of cuffs off his belt.

"Well played, Jason," Trane said, though he kept his eyes on Ellison and the other deputy. "Your father would be proud."

"Please, just shut the fuck up," I said.

As Kelly grabbed Trane's arms and pulled them behind his back, reciting the Miranda Act, Trane said, "Make me one promise: take care of Soledad. Like it or not, she's your blood, and now she's got nobody else."

Trane then spun around, breaking free of Kelly's grip before the deputy could get the cuffs on him. He head-butted Kelly, which sent the officer staggering back. Ellison went for his gun, as did Johannsen. I also went for mine, putting myself between Trane and Charley.

"Don't make another fucking move," Ellison barked out.

Trane ignored the warning. He grabbed the small suitcase, upended the table, and dove behind it, using it as cover as Johannsen and Ellison opened fire. Their bullets shattered the front window. Trane stood up from behind the table a second later, holding a Mac II subcompact machine gun in his hand. It must have been in the small suitcase. He sprayed the room with gunfire. As the bullets flew, I dove down on top of Charley to cover her body. Bullets from the barrage lifted Johannsen off his feet and threw him against the wall. Ellison kept shooting and hit Trane twice in the chest. Trane fell back, the machine gun still firing as he went down, spraying shrapnel into the ceiling.

I stood, my gun securely held in both hands, and approached with caution. I had to step past the overturned table to see Trane. He lay sprawled on his back, his mouth opening and closing, trying to take in air. Ellison's bullets had pierced one of his lungs. I moved around him, so I could kick the machine gun away.

"Captain!" Charley shouted. "Oh, Jesus. Jagger! Look!"

"Cover him," I told Kelly, meaning Trane, then I hurried to the other side of the table. The Captain lay on his back, his hands pressed against his throat. Blood flowed out past his fingers, across his neck and chest, and down onto the floor. He tried to speak but only a wet, garbled noise came out.

"Call for an ambulance," I told Kelly and dropped to my knees to apply more pressure on Ellison's wound. "Hold on, Captain. An ambulance is coming."

Ellison shook his head, his eyes wild. He clutched at my arm with a bloody hand. "No good," he managed to say.

"Stop, don't talk."

Ellison tried to say something else but couldn't form the words.

"Goddamn you," I said. "Don't you fucking die."

Ellison didn't listen. He couldn't hold on. I watched the life drift out of him as he clutched my arm and attempted to say goodbye. I felt lightheaded, as if I might keel over and pass out. Charley came and put a trembling hand on my shoulder. Looking up, I saw she was shivering, her teeth chattering—a combination of shock and the aftereffects of whatever drug Trane had given her. I stood, took off my jacket, and draped it over her shoulders.

"I'm sorry," she whispered. She looped her arm through mine and put her head against my arm as we stared down at the corpse of a man we both loved and respected.

"What's happened?" Soledad's voice came from behind us. I turned and saw her standing in the open doorway. She looked down at Ellison and gasped. "Oh, Lord." Her eyes searched the room until they found Trane. He was still alive but barely. His breath came out short and wheezing.

Rage came on strong, overtaking my shock and sadness. I wanted to go over and stomp his face into a mealy pulp. To smash his head in until he was dead. Instead, I pushed past my sister and exited the room to get away from the sight and stench of death.

"HEY, BEAUTIFUL," TRANE SAID, STARING UP AT SOLEDAD. SHE stood looming over him, like an angel come to carry him away. "Getting ... your wish. I'm dying." He struggled to get the words out.

"Yes, you are," she said.

"Tell me ... you still love me. Lie. Let me die hearing it."

"I always loved you, Colin." Her voice quivered. She had tears in her eyes. "But I was scared of you too."

Trane smiled weakly, nodding. He worked hard to swallow. "Why didn't you go away, then? Why stick around?"

"I didn't want to upset her life. To uproot her, the way I had been. I wanted her to know stability. And I knew if I had to kill you to keep you from taking that away, I would."

"Her?" Trane asked. "Who are you talking about?"

"Our daughter."

"Daughter," he whispered. "Ours?" His eyelids felt heavy. His breath grew shorter and harder to take in. "What's ... her name?"

"You'll never know."

Trane nodded. Soledad had saved the best for last—a final, devastating blow he would carry to the grave. "Tell her I'm sorry," he said and closed his eyes.

40

L ocal detectives and officers arrived. Trane held on long enough to tell them he had shot Captain Germaine Ellison. He admitted he had abducted and held hostage Charlotte Frasier after attempting to kill her and me in a fire at the Goleta cabin—where, he said, he also shot and killed a Santa Barbara detective and two police officers. He confessed to murdering Alex and Sylvia Davies, the Horton family, Eddie Gilmore, Chris Teller, and Evelyn Marbut. When Trane had finished, the detectives read him his rights, but we all knew it was a meaningless formality—he'd never make it to an arraignment. I doubted he would survive the ambulance ride to the hospital.

A second ambulance came and took Charley away, although she argued that she just wanted to go home to Los Angeles. "They have to check on you first," I'd told her. "I'll join you at the hospital as soon as I can get away. We'll head home together the minute the doctors give the go-ahead."

"Are you okay?" she asked. I told her I was handling it as best I could. "He was like a father to you," she said.

"More than that, he was a good friend," I said. "This is

the risk the job brings." I didn't tell her that I felt the weight of his death, the *guilt* of it, like a chain of pain thrown on my shoulders, and I didn't know how I could ever remove it.

"Thank you for saving my life," she said.

"I'm sorry I created a situation where I had to."

"It's the risk the job brings," Charley echoed. "And I love you for it." She touched her fingers to her burned lips, then put them against mine.

The paramedics drove off with her. Vanderbrook and his driver came and took the SUV—with Vanderbrook's money still inside. I didn't stop them or tell the local detectives who he was or what involvement he had in all that went down. As part of my arrangement with him, I let him go unscathed.

While we walked the Mojave detectives through the events of the shootout in the Desert Rose motel, our sheriff's deputies put Soledad in the back of their patrol cruiser and kept her there. Once the detectives were finished with me, I went to speak with her.

"What's going to happen to me now?" she asked.

"There's not a lot I can do to help you," I said.

"Am I going to jail?"

"That's not up to me to decide, Miss Varela. And I never like to guess about the outcome of a prosecutor's case."

Soledad paused, and then asked, "Do you think you'll ever be able to look at me as your sister?"

"I can't say. We could have avoided a lot of bad things if you'd just come to me from the beginning. Many people are dead now, including a man I knew and loved for a long time. For that, I'm not sure I can ever forgive you."

"I'm sorry."

"So am I."

"Can I tell you one last thing? Another story? About our

father?" I didn't answer, but I stayed in the cruiser seat, looking at her. "A week before he took his life, he came up to see me and Gina," she said. "It was on a weekend, a Saturday, so Gina was home."

"What do you mean? Your daughter doesn't live with you during the week?"

"That doesn't matter," she said. "It's not the point of the story."

"Okay."

"He took us to eat at this taqueria he loved."

"Super Rica," I said. "I know it."

"We had a good lunch. He was very caring toward Gina. He never let his hatred of Colin cloud or taint the way he looked at or treated his granddaughter. Or me, for that matter. Anyway, we drove down to the beach after to have ice cream and watch kites flying. While Gina played in the sand with another girl her age, I told Scotty that I'd learned about you. That I knew I had a half-brother who was a cop. Scotty grew quiet. I asked if he wanted us to meet. He shook his head. I thought he'd grown angry, but he said it wasn't because he was ashamed of me. He was ashamed of himself. He feared that if you learned about me, it would change the way you loved him. And that would be the worst thing that could ever happen. He said, 'Jason is the man I wish I could have been.' I responded by saying I didn't think someone was much of a man if he couldn't forgive his father for making a human mistake."

I didn't know what to say. I'm not sure she expected a response. She knew what she was doing. This message, via a sister my dad had not ever wanted me to know, was as close to an apology from the man as I would ever get. I wasn't sure if I hated him for all I'd learned these past days or if, to the contrary, it had all brought me closer to him. At least, now I understood the man better and more fully. He was flawed and weak, and—despite the evil and cruelty it now seemed he was capable of—that made him more human to me and less godlike.

THE DEPUTIES HEADED BACK WITH SOLEDAD TO LOS ANGELES. I stayed and filled in the blanks for the local PD. When I'd finished, I paid for a room in the motel and took a long shower. I had more than Captain Ellison's physical blood to wash off. Afterward, I drove to the hospital to check on Charley, calling Kathy in LA on the way. I kept vague about the events of the previous night and the morning, only telling her the case had taken a turn, and I might have to stay in Mojave for a day or two. I asked her how things had gone with Dr. Ryker.

"All is good," she told me. "You'll be happy." She wanted to wait to tell Charley and me the details when we were face to face. It was good to hear her sounding strong.

They had placed Charley in a private room at Lancaster Community Hospital, a small, one-story building on the western edge of town. I went searching for the doctor who examined her.

"There are fresh abrasions to already serious burns," the doctor told me, "and there's evidence of the beginnings of an infection. We've got her back on antibiotics."

"But she'll be okay?"

"I'll have a better prognosis tomorrow. She's going to need a lot of treatment and perhaps some skin grafting. But I believe she will recover just fine."

"That's good to hear. Thank you. Can I stay here with her?"

"She's sedated, so she'll most likely sleep straight

through till morning. You look like you could also use a good night's sleep. There's nothing you can really do here, so why don't you go home? We'll call you if there are any developments."

I hated leaving, but the doctor was right. There was nothing I could do other than sit with Charley, and she wouldn't even know I was there. I felt like I needed to spend some time with Kathy and tell her in person what had happened. I looked in on Charley, watching her sleep for a few minutes, and then left, heading back to LA.

I blasted "Out of the Angeles" by Amusement Parks on Fire, with all the windows open, as I drove home and tried not to think about Captain Ellison. The midday sun, music, and dry desert air filled the car with a heat I hoped would burn away my anger and disgust. But the images of Ellison's last moments alive chilled me like the remnants of a bad dream, while a litany of accusatory thoughts I couldn't hold off flooded my brain. *If I'd never agreed to take the case ... If I'd not called him to tell him about Charley's abduction ... If I'd not texted him on Vanderbrook's driver's phone, giving him the location of the hotel ... If I'd just given Trane the money and let him escape ...*

A dozen ways Ellison's death might have been avoided, all meaningless now. And if I were facing his ghost, he'd probably tell me I'd made the right call. The *only* call. There was no guarantee Trane wouldn't have killed Charley if he had the chance. "If my death ensured her survival," Ellison would say, "then it was a successful plan."

His ghost would be right. I would have gladly taken that bullet to save her. I wished like hell that's the way it had gone down. Me, instead of Ellison. Me, instead of this man I loved like a father.

I PULLED INTO MY DRIVEWAY JUST AFTER TWO IN THE afternoon. Kathy's car was parked at the curb. I could hear music, Jay-Z, coming from her room as I entered the house. I knocked on her door.

"Don't freak out," I called to her. "It's me. I'm back early."

"Hey," she said as I stepped in. "I thought you had to stay in Mojave for a couple days."

"Plans changed. I came home to see you. I'll be going up again tonight."

"Is Charley okay?"

"She will be," I said and sat on the corner of her bed.

Kathy pushed up to a sitting position, shutting her computer and shoving it to the side.

"What does that mean?" she asked.

"I didn't want to go into details on the phone. There was a fire at the Goleta cabin, and Charley was hurt. She's recovering in a Mojave hospital. She's going to be okay. Don't worry about that."

"How did the fire happen?"

"Someone from Pop's old unit, a very bad man, started it to hurt Charley and me. He's dead now."

"Did you kill him?"

"No, Captain Ellison did. He died protecting us."

I told her the rest of the story. I held nothing back.

"Oh, Jesus. Dad, I'm so sorry. You must be freaking out. Captain Ellison was like a second father to you."

"Yeah, he sure was. And a good friend."

"And Charley ... God." Kathy paused. "I'm going with you, back up to Mojave. I want to see her, be with her. Charley needs as much love around her as we can offer."

I didn't argue. I gave my daughter a crushing hug.

WE WENT TO LUNCH AT GOLDEN APPLE, A LITTLE CHINESE restaurant we both liked in Studio City, and as we ate chicken lo mein and Kung Pao shrimp, Kathy told me about her session with Dr. Anna Ryker. Kathy was impressed with the psychiatrist's unorthodox method, her laid-back demeanor, and especially her mixture of yoga and breathing techniques with one-on-one therapy.

"She told me I should learn transcendental meditation," Kathy said. "Like you did."

"I've been saying that for months."

"I know, but it took hearing it from a professional for it to sink in."

"No worries. Whatever it takes to get you into it. We can go next weekend if they've got an available space. It's four sessions over as many days, a few hours each time."

"Can we afford it? Dr. Ryker said it isn't cheap."

"We'll manage. This is important, and it's going to help you. It's a worthwhile investment."

"Also, she thinks I should come see her twice a week, at least for the first few months. She said you should call her to work out some sort of payment arrangement. Is that okay?"

"Of course. I'm happy you think it's going to work."

"She's really nice. I met her daughters too."

"Janis and Billie?"

"Yeah, you know them?"

"No, she just talked about them."

"They're total opposites. The older one, Janis, is wild and outgoing. Billie's a bit more goth. But they're both cool. Janis thinks we should hang out."

"That'd be nice."

"Not weird that their mom is my therapist?"

"I think Anna, Janis, and Billie can handle it. And you too."

Kathy went quiet, pushing food around on her plate. When she looked back up, she had tears in her eyes. They came on instantly, without warning. "Charley's gonna be okay, right?"

"Yes, definitely. I have no doubt."

"I feel guilty."

"Why?" I asked.

"I pushed her to go with you because I didn't want either of you hovering while I got ready to see Dr. Ryker."

"Don't do that," I said. "This is in no way your fault, Katbird. None of us knew how this would play out. If anything, I'm the one who should take the rap. I've been pushing Charley to get back in the game for months. I thought if she tagged along on this case, she might recapture some of the mojo she loved about being a cop. I'm to blame for this, nobody else."

It was yet more guilt I'd be living with for a very long time.

41

B ack home, I contacted the West Hollywood Division to find out what they'd done with Soledad. There was no credible evidence tying her to the murders of Armando Trujillo, Karl Unger, or the police officers, so the assistant DA cut her loose.

Next, I phoned Dan Griffin, the manager of the Mar Vista Apartments, and asked if he could find out if Miss Varela had returned to her apartment.

"I don't need to find out for you," Dan said. "I already know. She's upstairs now. She got home about an hour ago."

"Have you ever seen her with a little girl?" I asked.

"Sure, Gina. That's her daughter."

"Does Gina live with Soledad?"

"No, she's enrolled in a private school up near Santa Maria. I don't remember the name of it. Soledad pays a family to take care of her during the week and goes up on Friday nights and stays the weekend."

Today was Friday. I could be in Santa Barbara in less than two hours. But to what end? What was there left to say? Learning about Soledad's daughter conflicted me. My half-sister might be guilty of conspiracy to murder, even if she hadn't pulled the trigger herself, and there was no evidence she'd arranged the killings. But sending her to jail would orphan an eight-year-old girl. Did I want to destroy another life? I'd come back to the job, to the department, at Ellison's request, and I'd tried to do my job as best I could. Now the captain was dead, and the woman I loved lay in a hospital room with serious burns over most of her body. Did I really want to go three for three?

Finally, I called Anna Ryker and thanked her for seeing Kathy on such short notice.

"She's a strong and wonderful young woman," Anna said. "I can't talk about our session, but I can tell you that my sense is she'll come out of this okay."

"That's the best news I've heard in a while."

"How are you?" she asked. "You sound ... I don't know ... sad."

"Someone I cared for very much died this morning."

"I'm sorry, Jason." Anna hesitated, then added, "Do you want to come in and talk about it? I've got some time this afternoon, around four, if you'd like."

Hearing her say this, I realized it was the main reason I'd called. I needed to talk about what had happened and what I was thinking and feeling. And I needed to do it with someone I knew would understand without judgment.

ANNA'S HAIR WAS SHORTER THAN WHEN I'D LAST SEEN HER, during the murder investigation with which she'd helped me, and the wisps of gray in it were more pronounced. She wore a Mexican beach blouse, faded jeans, and sandals. Jade earrings matched a necklace visible between the open buttons of her blouse.

"I had an epiphany as I drove here," I told her, sitting in her home office of cream-colored furniture. We each held a mug of green tea sweetened with honey, and I stared out a large window at a Topanga canyon sky so dazzling and clear it seemed artificial, like an image from a film. "The truth came at me so strongly that it overwhelmed me. I had to stop driving and pull the car to the side of the road."

"I'm glad you did. I'd hate for you to have had an accident in the middle of a revelation." We both smiled. "Go on."

"I think my passion for what I do, a passion I've carried for more years than I can remember, died with learning the truth about my father and the murder of Captain Ellison. I don't know if I can ever go back to that world."

"What are you saying exactly?"

"I don't think I can be a cop any longer."

"Do you think maybe that's a knee-jerk reaction?" Anna said. "Perhaps spurred by anger and sadness? It could just be that you need some time off."

"I've done that already. After Kathy's rape. Two months' worth." I set the mug down on crocheted coaster atop a mahogany end table. "This case was my return."

"Okay, so how does this new decision make you feel?"

"I don't know. Scared. I've only ever known the world of police work. My father was a vice cop. I went into law enforcement because of him."

"It's okay to be scared of a decision."

I crossed my legs and clasped my fingers together. "I learned over the course of this last case that he was about as corrupt as they come."

"Does learning that change the way you view *your* life?"

"Yes, I suppose it does. It changes the way I view him. Things trickle down, right?"

"I don't buy into the notion that the sins of the father will be visited upon the son. 'The righteousness of the righteous will be upon himself,'" Anna quoted, "'and the wickedness of the wicked will be upon himself.'"

"Ezekiel." I looked down at my hands, fearful I might still see Ellison's bloodstains on them. "I'm far from righteous."

"Do you feel you're wicked? Have you done corrupt things?"

"I shot the man who raped my daughter, though he wasn't aiming a gun at me. Over the course of that same investigation, I allowed a woman to go free, though she tortured and killed a bad man in cold blood. And just this morning, I decided not to pursue the arrest of my half-sister, though I have every reason to believe she ordered the killing of two people to keep her identity a secret."

"Those are troubling actions," Anna said.

"And then some." Only after I said this did I remember it was a favorite phrase of Ellison's.

"I imagine in your line of work you often face questions of morality and correct conduct," Anna said, "without time for reflection or debate."

"That's the thing. There should always be time for it, even if you're dealing in life-and-death situations. Especially in those times."

She shifted in her chair, pulling her legs up under her. "How's the meditation going?"

"It helps. Kathy seems interested, and that pleases me."

"I want to know about you."

"I've had trouble keeping up with it lately. Things have been crazy, and I've had no schedule. It's hard when I'm on a case. I'm eager to get back to a routine."

"Maybe that's all you need. To get back to a routine."

"What I need is a new routine," I said.

"Don't you think you've done a lot of good as a detective? Despite these recent ... detours, for want of a better word."

"Yes, but I'm questioning my judgment now. I've seen it happen enough times. I imagine it's what happened with my old man. You talk about detours. That's the right word, actually. Some cops, they start down a road, make a turn, and suddenly, they're on another road, a darker one but too far along to turn back. I don't want to become that guy."

"So don't," she said. "Nothing is predestined. Everything we do is by choice."

"And sometimes," I said, "our choice is to give up."

AFTER LEAVING ANNA, I DROVE TO WEST HOLLYWOOD, AND I stopped at the Laurel Avenue house. Standing in the ruins of the kitchen, staring at a charred table that had belonged to the Hortons, placed in the same spot we put ours in when we lived there, I thought about the night I found my dad dead from a bullet wound to the head.

"You fucking coward!" I shouted to the empty room. Tears welled up in my eyes. I wiped them away with the back of my sleeve. "Why couldn't you talk to me? Maybe I could've helped you. Maybe I could've stopped you. You didn't need to carry this alone."

I sank down onto one of the burned chairs. It felt wobbly under my weight, but I didn't care. I whispered, "Now, everything's changed."

42

NOVEMBER 16, 2010—SC PERSONAL FILES. NOT FOR OFFICIAL EYES

Maybe I've got no choice but to tell Jason everything. Once the grand jury hands down indictments, there's no telling how far things could go. Or how deep the feds will end up digging. I'm probably not as safe as I've told myself I am. I've tried to behave like a man shocked by the deception because that's what stunned men do. I've fought the allegations against my team and raised a stink because a cop who rolls over too easily looks suspicious. I've talked with the team in private. They don't want to see an old man like me die in prison. They'll take the heat, they say. I want to believe them. Except Parker, of course. He knows the deal. I can see it in his eyes. It's still hard for me to get used to Soledad being part of my life, but no way can I ever accept him being a part of hers. So let him hate me. Like I give a damn.

I don't know what Jason's going to think. I hope he'll keep the truth from Kathy. At least for now. I remember the shock and disappointment I felt when I first found out my old man was a gambler and a womanizer. It's not something you take in well, *even as an adult. Hell, maybe Jason already suspects what I am. What I've done. He's a good cop, better than I ever was. It wouldn't surprise me to learn he's already figured things out.*

I love my son. I swore when he was born I'd never do anything to hurt or disappoint him. Ironic, the bullshit we tell ourselves, isn't it? I spent my whole life doing just the opposite. Now, here I am, looking down the barrel of a sinful life. I'm a coward except when dealing with other cowards. That's about the only time I find strength. By confronting scum. The lowlifes. It gives me a chance to pretend I'm better.

Jason's brave, and he's honest, God bless him. There's no gray area for him, at least not that I can see. No ambiguity in his code. It's pure. Clean. I don't think he'll ever let anything corrupt it. Nothing like his old man. I'm a faithless fool who couldn't stick to the path I chose.

Fuck, it hurts to look at the truth. Sometimes, I think it's not worth facing anymore.

I LOOKED UP FROM READING THE JOURNAL ON MY STUDY DESK and saw Kathy standing in the open doorway.

"Hey, Katbird. What's up?"

"You okay, Dad? Why are you crying?"

"Am I?" I reached up, touched my cheek. My fingers came away damp. "It's nothing. Just some stuff my dad wrote."

"You want me to leave you alone?"

"No, I need a break."

"When do you want to head back to Mojave?"

I looked at my watch. It was just after 8 p.m. "It's kind of late, and Charley will sleep through the night. How about first thing in the morning? That way she'll be in better condition for visitors. And I'd like to keep reading. I'm almost to the end of Pop's journals. I think I may have just figured something out."

Kathy kissed me and said goodnight. I asked her to close the door as she left. I sat back in the chair, staring at the multitude of black-and-white journals spread haphazardly across the desk.

It had been there, right in front of me, the whole time. In the books. His journals. In the words but not the content. Taking each book individually, you'd never spot it. Only reading through them in sequence, beginning to end, did the clues gel. Or rather, the clue. Singular. One big one only I could decipher.

The dates of the entries were the keys. Each log, starting with the one in June 2010 (when he wrote about the decision to target Yuri Petrov), had been written three days from the previous entry. Every single one. Methodical. Exact. Three days—a log. Another three days—another one. It didn't matter how much time actually should have passed for the events to make sense in sequence. He'd wait three days, then make another log. This would go on like clockwork for three months. Then, there would be a month with no entries at all. Silence for four or five weeks. Followed by three more months of logs, each again three days apart. Three months on at three-day intervals, then one month off.

It was the pattern of a puzzle my father invented. A numbers game he often played with me when I was an adolescent. In the puzzle, you worked backwards. Start with a sum, then figure out what you need to do to create a method to arrive at that sum. Then create a code.

I added up the number of months from June 2010 until the end April 2011, when Yuri's arrest was made. It came to eleven months. Nothing was written in September or January, leaving three sets of three months' activity. Nine months total: June/July/August—one month of thirty days and two of thirty-one. Add this all up and it equaled 92. Divide by three. The sum was 30.66. I did the same with October/November/December. 30.66. February/March/April totaled eighty-nine days. Divided by three: 29.66. Add it all up: 90.98. Then divide again the final sum by three: 30.32.

Evelyn Marbut—Dad's housekeeper for the Goleta cabin, Colin Parker's eighth victim—lived at 3032 Valerio Road.

I WENT INTO KATHY'S ROOM AND TOLD HER I NEEDED TO drive to Santa Barbara before I could go back to Mojave; something had come up that needed my immediate response. I'd leave now and hopefully return by morning.

"Everything okay?" she asked.

"Yeah, I just need to wrap up a few things."

Kathy grew quiet.

"It's nothing dangerous," I said. "Colin Parker is dead. Everyone connected to my father and his old crew who could pose a threat to me is out of the picture."

"I know." Still, she looked concerned. Misinterpreting her, I asked if she was nervous spending the night alone.

"No, Dad, come on. I've been alone for two nights already. I'm just eager to check on Charley, and you might get delayed. What if you have to stay up there longer? How about I head to Mojave on my own first thing in the morning? You can meet me there."

I couldn't think of any reason why Kathy shouldn't go on without me. "Okay, it's an easy drive up the 405 and the 14 for you. Couple of hours, depending on traffic."

"I'll be fine," she said.

"You need to be prepared, though, for when you get

there, seeing Charley alone. The burns look bad. They'll heal. She's going to be all right. But go in knowing it'll be a shock. I say this, so you won't freak out, and I don't want Charley to feel uncomfortable by your reaction."

"I'll be strong. Promise."

"I know you will." I hugged Kathy and kissed her forehead, then headed back north for the second time since I'd been pulled into this nightmare.

It was a clear, smooth drive to Santa Barbara, with Shawn Colvin's *Whole New You* album keeping me company. I played the music loud, Shawn's haunting voice singing about sadness and new beginnings. The darkness and emptiness of the barren stretches between the towns comforted me almost as much as the music.

I had an idea what I'd find in Evelyn Marbut's house, but I knew the clues in the journal were meant for me. To my knowledge, only my dad and I ever did his numbers game. He must have assumed we would never move away from the Laurel Avenue home, and one day, I would clean out that old trunk and see the false bottom. I imagine he wanted me to learn about his secrets and crimes only after he was dead. But my father was also sending me to Evelyn's home for a reason.

I REACHED HER PLACE JUST AFTER MIDNIGHT. IT WAS DARK inside and out. As my headlights flashed across the decrepit façade, I thought of those empty houses at the end of the street in every horror movie I ever saw as a child. Evelyn's house was haunted too. They say ghosts hang around to complete unfinished business. Did Evelyn know about my father's dark side? Would her ghost be inside now to guide me to whatever secret he hid in her home?

There was no crime scene tape across the front door—the detectives and forensic team had done their work and left. I jumped the side fence as I'd done days before, walked to the back of the house, and entered the kitchen through a back door whose lock I had to pick this time. A peculiar smell hit me as I walked through the kitchen and into the living room: a scent of ghosts and lingering death.

"Evelyn, are you here?" I asked of the darkness. I heard only silence at first. Then came the tinkling of wind chimes from the front porch. As good a sign as any. "Okay, where do I start?"

She had no answer for that.

I went through the house room by room, closet by closet, drawer by drawer, box by box. Had this been Trane's method in the other homes? A careful search before frustration set in, leading him to tear down walls and rip up floors? I had no plans to go that far. I wouldn't destroy anything. "And I promise I won't burn your house down," I told Evelyn's spirit.

I didn't need to. I found what I was looking for in the garage, barely hidden. He had put it in a large trunk that sat against the back wall, similar to the one where he had stashed his journals, not even covered by a tarp. I had to snap open the lock, but that was easily done with one twist of a screwdriver. Inside: packets of hundred-dollar bills, neatly stacked, each totaling ten thousand dollars. Four hundred packets, in all.

Four million dollars.

He gave half a million to Soledad, she said. Another half a million he spent on God knows what. Or perhaps he gave it to Evelyn, or she took it of her own volition. Had he intended for the rest to go to Kathy and me? There were no instructions in the trunk. And, to my relief, there were no kilos of heroin.

Just four million dollars in cash.

"I knew all along he'd taken it." The voice, a woman's, came from behind me in the open garage door. I turned, expecting to see Soledad, figuring she'd been following me since I returned to Los Angeles.

Instead, I saw Paula Ramirez standing there. Two men in leather jackets flanked her. Both had guns in their hands, pointed at me. "And I knew you'd figure out where it was hidden," she said. "It's good thing prison taught me to be patient." She smiled. "Now step away from the trunk, Jason, nice and easy, and clasp your hands behind your head."

43

I did as Paula told me, stepping away from the trunk filled with cash, lacing my hands behind my head as I did.

"How long have you been watching me?" I asked.

"How long do you think? It was easier than I expected. You had that rich guy on your ass, and that was your focus." Paula meant Vanderbrook. I'd been so aware of his tail that I never spotted Paula or her people. It meant she had been surveilling me for some time. "And that nightmare with Trane. I'm sorry about Charlotte. She going to be okay?"

"Time will tell. I hope so."

"I knew eventually you'd lead me here," she said.

"Who are they?" I nodded toward the goons at her side.

"It doesn't matter. Just guys, here to help me take the money. It's not like you can just put five million in a carry-on bag."

"Only four million. Dad gave some of it away."

Paula shrugged. "Thieves can't be picky. Let's not make this difficult, okay?"

She stayed put while the two men approached. One

frisked me and took my gun. The other removed a roll of heavy-duty trash bags from his pocket and began to pull off individual ones from it. He laid them out, side by side, on the floor of the garage, next to the trunk.

"Maybe I should've pressed assault charges against you," I said to Paula.

"They'd never have stuck."

"No, probably not. But maybe it would've slowed you down."

"Don't worry. I plan to leave you with a cut. It is your father's cash."

"No, it's money he stole from someone else."

"Yeah, from Yuri Petrov, a drug dealing scumbag. *Ladron que roba ladron tiene cien años de perdon*." It was the same phrase I'd heard Trujillo use. A thief who robs a thief gets a hundred-year pardon. It seemed an even more foolish phrase now, coming from her.

"I was beginning to fear the money was a myth," she said. "A legend. No one but Trane ever even claimed to have seen it."

"But I have," I said. "It's real to me now. As is my father's criminality."

"Nobody wanted you to ever know about that, especially not Scotty." As she talked, the men removed the packets of money from the trunk and put them into the thick, black plastic bags.

"No, you're wrong," I said. "He did. He left a confession. I just found it later than he thought I would."

"Well, I'm sorry you know the truth. But you're a big boy. You can handle it."

"Can I ask you something? Who ordered the hit on Trujillo?"

Paula seemed troubled by the question. "Someone who

needed him out of the way, obviously. I guess we'll never know for sure," she said.

"I think I do." Paula was responsible, not Soledad. She had Armando killed to finish off the team. The attack while we were interrogating her was simply a means to get away, so she could follow me around without any pressure, hoping I would lead her to my father's hidden stash. And she found a way to hack into my father's account, to make it look as if Soledad arranged payment to the hitman.

"Trane was looking in all the wrong places," Paula said. "He should've started with you."

"It would have saved a lot of bloodshed." My shoulders had started to ache. I lowered my arms. Paula didn't seem to care. "Just tell me Soledad wasn't behind it," I said. "That's all I care about knowing."

"Don't worry. Soledad is as innocent as you are." Still no admission of guilt from Paula. "And just so you know, I never expected you'd come talk to me at the apartment. Or the other detective, Unger. Just bad luck that you showed up when you did."

"Yeah," I said. "Bad luck, all around."

The men put the last of the cash into the bags, six in all. They secured each with a zip tie, then lifted two bags apiece, and carried them off toward the street. Paula picked up the fifth one.

"The last is for you," she said.

"I don't want it."

She smiled. "You'll change your mind. Everybody does. It's human nature."

I watched her walk away, out of the security light of the backyard and into the darkness of the front. Several car doors slammed shut, then an engine turned over. I ran after, hoping to get the license plate and call it in, but by the time I got to the street, they'd driven away.

I COUNTED THE REMAINING MONEY. SIX HUNDRED AND FIFTY thousand dollars. Enough to buy anyone a new life. Even me. As much as I needed a fresh start—and as tempting as the cash looked, stacked across the backseat of the Jeep as I added it up—this was money amassed from death and abuse. The search for it had cost a lot of innocent people their lives. Including Captain Ellison. I refused to benefit from it.

Instead, I drove to the Mar Vista. Soledad's third-floor apartment windows were dark. Most likely, she'd already gone to Santa Maria to be with her daughter. I woke Dan Griffin and had him open Soledad's apartment door. Inside, I left the six hundred and fifty thousand dollars in the bag, its plastic sheen looking like coal against the white apartment wall. For Soledad, perhaps this *would* be a diamond in the rough. I also left a note: *'Colin Parker killed many people to get this. There's too much blood on it for me to keep it. Use it for your daughter and yourself, or give it to charity. It's your call.'*

44

By the time I arrived in Mojave, the sun was a quarter of the way up in the sky, lighting the distant mountains with a purple hue. Kathy had left before dawn to make the drive. I spotted her red Yaris parked near the main entrance of the hospital. I stopped beside it and let the War on Drugs song, "Lost in the Dream," finish before shutting off the engine.

Kathy sat waiting in the triage anteroom. "Charley's in treatment," she said as I approached. "I just got here. We'll be able to see her in twenty minutes."

"Did you get any breakfast?" I asked.

Kathy shook her head.

"I'm famished. Let's hit the cafeteria."

We sat near a window that looked out over an enclosed desert garden of cactus, sage, and yellow bells. I ate a not-very-good breakfast burrito and drank two cups of coffee. Kathy had a fruit salad.

"What happened in Santa Barbara?" she asked. "Something bad? You look troubled."

"I'd rather not go into details." I pushed away the plate. "Just that the case is closed."

"Good." She speared a piece of melon but didn't lift her fork to eat. "I'm sorry about Captain Ellison. You're blaming yourself, aren't you?"

I looked out into the garden. A chameleon darted across the sand, onto a smooth rock, and then froze. "Yeah, I am."

"He wouldn't want you to."

"I know. Still ..." I drank some coffee.

"What?"

"I don't think I can go back."

"Home?"

"No, to the job. It was a mistake for me to try."

"You just weren't ready."

"It's more than that," I said. "I'm still trying to process things. When I've had time to, I'll be able to explain my feelings more clearly."

"Okay. Whatever you want to do, I'll accept it."

"Thank you."

"What will you do instead?"

I laughed without humor. "I don't know."

"Are we going to be okay?"

"Yeah, we'll be fine."

And I wanted to believe that was the truth.

CHARLEY SMILED AND HELD A HAND OUT TO KATHY AS WE entered her room. She didn't seem embarrassed by the burns Kathy saw for the first time, and Kathy didn't seem shocked. I stayed by the door as they said their hellos, and Kathy bombarded her with questions related to the fire and the abduction. Wanting to give them space to speak freely, I smiled at Charley, then slipped back out.

It was another warm desert morning. A pair of orderlies sat on a bench near the parking lot, smoking and talking. Someone waiting in a car nearby had the radio on, a jazz piece playing. Something familiar, a tune I must have heard my father listen to often enough for it to stay in my memory. Coltrane, I think. A woman's name was the title, an odd one —beautiful, like the song. It came to me eventually: "Naima." And with the name came a memory of my dad talking about the song. How beautiful he found it, how it often made him cry. He told me Coltrane had named it for his wife.

I never loved jazz the way my father did. And he always criticized my musical taste. He told me rock-and-roll burned too hard from the beginning, leaving it nowhere to go, but jazz took its time and allowed the listener to get lost. That notion proved true, in my dad's case. He and Colin Parker got lost in the minor chords.

Soledad could go either way. I wanted to believe she would save herself, for her daughter's sake. The thing that makes us good is our ability not to be bad. We're the only species on the planet that knows its own mortality, and I'd be willing to bet we're also the only species that knows how to choose between good and evil. Strong or weak. Faithful or faithless. We decide. And in that choice, we find our humanity or our desperation. Captain Ellison lived at one end of that spectrum; my father, at the other.

I landed somewhere in the middle. And I felt lost. I had no idea what I needed to do to redefine my life and give me purpose again. Sometimes, it's okay not to know. Sometimes, you find yourself—your identity—while you are on the journey to figure it all out.

The song in the car ended, replaced by some blaring, frenetic piece of hard bop that made me uncomfortable. I walked away from it, hurrying back across the lot and into the hospital.

In the triage anteroom, my cell phone buzzed, a number I didn't recognize.

"Jason Chance," I said, answering.

"This is Jensen Vanderbrook." His voice sounded older and more tired than when we last spoke. "You don't need to say anything, just listen. I found the woman you told me about, Greta Klingner. The one who was involved with JoJo Sellars and my son. It wasn't hard. Her yacht *Amadeus* was moored off the coast of Viña del Mar, in Chile. I had men visit her. She confessed to killing Derek. They say she seemed relieved to finally get it all out. When pressed about your involvement, she told them she'd tried to get you to shoot Derek, but you refused."

Vanderbrook paused, clearing his throat. "I wanted answers. I wanted to know the truth. Now, I do. I learned some ugly things about my son in the process. I understand you've had a similar experience regarding your father."

"Yes, that's true," I said.

"I'm sorry. This squares us, Mr. Chance. Goodbye."

Vanderbrook ended the call. I slipped my phone into my jacket, glancing over at the nurse's station where Kathy stood, asking an orderly for some fresh drinking water for Charley. She didn't see me. I left her there and went into Charley's room.

Charley smiled when she saw me and held out her hand. I sat by the bed and took it.

"Marry me," I whispered, staring into her eyes. "I don't ever *not* want you in my life." I leaned in and kissed her burned lips. When I pulled back, I saw tears in her eyes. She nodded once.

And that was enough.

AFTERWORD

I hope you enjoyed this Jason Chance mystery. Please consider reviewing TORCH SONGS FOR THE DEAD on Amazon. I love reading your thoughts, and honest reviews help other readers as they make that all-important decision to read a book (or not). Long or short, whatever you feel, I'll appreciate it. Thank you so much!

Jason Chance returns in THE BAD SIDE OF GOOD.

ACKNOWLEDGMENTS

As always, my ever-loving thanks to:
Adriana, my first and best reader, always.
My daughters, Alana and Laura, for their wonderful
support.
The Los Angeles Count Sheriff's Department.
The California cities of Los Angeles, Santa Barbara, Goleta,
and Mojave.
And, as always, a HUGE thanks to you, Dear Reader, for
taking these journeys with Jason, Charley, Kathy, Captain
Ellison, and me.

39621100R00146

Made in the USA
Lexington, KY
21 May 2019